Karin Tidbeck

Jagannath

Karin Tidbeck is the author of the novel *Amatka* and the short story collection *Jagannath*, which was awarded the James Tiptree, Jr. Award and the Crawford Award, as well as shortlisted for the World Fantasy Award. Originally from Stockholm, Sweden, she lives and works in Malmö as a free-lance writer, translator, and creative-writing teacher and writes fiction in Swedish and English. She devotes her spare time to forteana, subversive cross-stitching, and Nordic LARP.

Jagannath

Jagannath

· · · · · · · *stories* · · ·

KARIN TIDBECK

VINTAGE BOOKS
A Division of Penguin Random House LLC
New York

CONTENTS

Elizabeth Hand

It's rare, almost unheard of, to encounter an author so extraordinarily gifted she appears to have sprung full-blown into the literary world, like Athena from the head of Zeus. But we live in extraordinary times, and with Karin Tidbeck we appear to have gotten the artist our times deserve.

A hundred years ago, the great fantasist Lord Dunsany wrote of the world beyond the fields we know. With the ascent of fantasy as the dominant popular literary form of the early twenty-first century, we've seen that world grow increasingly gentrified, commodified, and mainstreamed. This is a long way of saying that when it comes to speculative fiction, it takes a lot to surprise me. I can't think of when I last read a collection that blew me away the way that *Jagannath* has, or one that's left me somewhat at a loss to describe just how strange and beautiful and haunting these tales are.

Of course, Tidbeck's appearance on the literary scene isn't quite as sudden as it seems to me. She's been publishing for more than a decade, and many of the stories contained herein first appeared in her native Sweden, where they were collected in *Vem är Arvid Pekon?* English translations of several of these tales have been published in U.S. and U.K. magazines and anthologies. In 2010 she attended the prestigious Clarion Writers' Workshop, a longtime proving ground for writers who have gone on to become major voices in the field. She's also one of the few writers of the fantastic to have received a grant from the Swedish Authors' Fund.

Yet there's still something startling about the presence of so many remarkable pieces in such a deceptively slender volume. In its feverish intensity and sublimely estranging effects, her work sometimes evokes that of James M. Tiptree, Jr. (Alice Sheldon); in particular, "Aunts" and the title story can hold their own with Tiptree's classic depiction of alien consciousness, "Love Is the Plan the Plan Is Death."

But Tidbeck's writing is more generous and far more emotionally engaged than Tiptree's. Even when the inexplicable occurs, as it does throughout these tales, a reader responds as Tidbeck's characters do, with an underlying empathy. Their sense of loss or astonishment or melancholy resignation never trumps the deeper sense of recognition that, as Hamlet observed, there are more things in heaven and earth than are dreamt of in our philosophy. As in "Augusta Prima," where the title character asks,

"I have to know . . . What is the nature of the world?"

The djinneya smiled with both rows of teeth. "Which one?"

In a 2012 interview with *Strange Horizons,* Tidbeck spoke of the crepuscular (real) world where she lives in Sweden:

We spend a lot of time in twilight, which is a liminal condition, a no-man's-land. The light has an eerie and melancholy quality. I suppose this has carried over into my writing as well, both in the sense of the eerie and melancholy, but also the sensation of having stepped sideways into another world where the sun has stopped in its course.

This liminal sense of transcending borders holds true for all the stories in *Jagannath*, which span folktale, fantasy, magic realism, science fiction, and, in "Pyret," a Borgesian taxonomy of an imaginary creature. Many of these tales are disturbing; they are also darkly funny and, to this American's sensibility at least, genuinely strange. Tidbeck shares with the great Robert Aickman a gift for invoking a profound sense of disassociation from the world we think we know, pointing us toward a breach through which any number of unimaginable things might (and do) emerge. More than anything, there is a palpable *absence* in many of her stories: of loved ones (especially parents); of the passage of time; of knowledge of the very world the characters inhabit.

Still, nature abhors a vacuum, even in a parallel plane of existence, and unforeseen things emerge to fill that void. "Reindeer Mountain," perhaps my favorite of all the stories collected here, is a tour de force of the uncanny. "Who Is Arvid Pekon?" may make you reluctant to ever pick up a telephone again, and "Brita's Holiday Village" reminds one how unsettling a resort in the off-season can be. The narrator of "Cloudberry Jam" recounts a conversation with the creature she has made in a tin can:

"Why did you make me?" you said.

"I made you so that I could love you," I said.

Similarly, Karin Tidbeck has written these stories so that readers may love them. I certainly do. And I suspect you will, too.

Jagannath

Beatrice

FRANZ HILLER, a physician, fell in love with an airship. He was visiting a fair in Berlin to see the wonders of the modern age that were on display: automobiles, propeller planes, mechanical servants, difference engines, and other things that would accompany man into the future.

The airship was moored in the middle of the aviation exhibit. According to the small sign by the cordon, her name was Beatrice.

In contrast to the large commercial airships, Beatrice is built for a maximum of two passengers. An excellent choice for those who live far from public airship masts or do not wish to be crowded in with strangers. Manufacturing will start soon. Order yours today, from Lefleur et Fils!

Franz had had no previous interest in airships. He had never seen one up close, let alone traveled in one. Neither had he any interest in love. At thirty, he was still a bachelor; his prospects were good, but he had been profoundly disinterested in any potential wives his parents had presented to him. His mother was becoming more and more insistent, and sooner or later Franz would have to make up his mind. But then he found himself here, in Berlin, facing this airship: Beatrice, her name tolling like a bell.

Franz couldn't stop looking at her. Her body was a voluptuous oblong, matte skin wrapped tightly over a gently rounded skeleton. The little gondola was made of dark wood (*finest mahogany!*) and embellished with brass details (*every part hand-wrought!*), with thick glass windows that rounded at the edges. Inside, the plush seats were embroidered with French lilies, facing an immaculately polished console. Beatrice was perfect. She bobbed in a slow up-down motion, like a sleeping whale. But she was very much awake. Franz could feel her attention turn to him and remain there, the heat of her sightless gaze.

He came back the next day, and the next, just to look at Beatrice and feel her gaze upon him. They could never touch; he once tried to step inside the cordon but was brusquely reprimanded by the guards. Franz could sense the same want from her that filled him, a longing to be touched.

He sought out the representative of Lefleur et Fils, Lefleur the younger, in fact: a thin man with oil-stained fingers who looked uncomfortable in his suit. Franz offered to buy Beatrice outright; he would write a check on the spot, or pay in cash if needed. Out of the question, Lefleur the younger replied. That airship there was a prototype. Not at any price? Not at any price. How could they start manufacture without the prototype? Of course, Monsieur Hiller was welcome to order an airship, just not this one.

Franz didn't dare explain why he wanted the prototype so badly. He accepted the catalog offered to him and returned home. He thought of Beatrice while caressing her picture in the catalog. Her smooth skin, her little gondola. How he wanted to climb into her little gondola.

After two weeks, the fair closed. Beatrice was taken home to Lefleur et Fils' factory in Paris. Franz fantasized about traveling to the factory, breaking into it at night, and stealing her; or pleading his case to the owners, who would be so touched by his story that they would let go of her. Franz did none of this. Instead, he moved out of his parents' home, much to their consternation, and left for Berlin, where he found new employment and rented a warehouse on Stahlwerkstrasse. Then he placed an order.

Two months later, a transport arrived at the warehouse on Stahlwerkstrasse. Four burly men who didn't speak a word of German unloaded four enormous boxes and proceeded to unpack the various parts of a small airship. When they left, an exact copy of Beatrice was moored in the warehouse.

The realization dawned on Franz, as he stood alone in the warehouse studying his airship. This new Beatrice was disinterested. She hovered quietly in the space without a trace of warmth. Franz walked along her length. He stroked her skin with a hand. It was cool. He traced the smooth, polished mahogany of her gondola with his fingers, breathing in the aroma of fresh wood and varnish. Then he opened the little door and gingerly seated himself inside, where a musky undertone mingled with the smells of copper and fresh rubber. He imagined that it was Beatrice. He summoned the sensation of warm cushions receiving him, how she dipped under his weight. But this Beatrice, Beatrice II, had a seat with firm stuffing that didn't give.

"We'll manage," said Franz to the console. "We'll manage. You can be my Beatrice. We'll get used to each other."

Anna Goldberg, a printer's assistant, fell in love with a steam engine. She was the youngest and ugliest daughter in a well-to-do family in Hamburg; her father owned one of the largest printing works in the country. Since Anna showed intellectual talent, she was allowed schooling and worked for her father as his secretary. In that way she would at least earn her keep. Anna was happy with her employment, but not because she loved the art of printing or the art of being a secretary. It was the printing presses. When other girls her age mooned over boys, she had a violent crush on a Koenig & Bauer. However, it wouldn't do to start a romance openly in front of her father. She saved every pfennig of her income, so that when the day came she could afford to follow her love. At twenty-eight, she was still waiting for the right opportunity.

It finally came the day she met Hercules at the Berlin fair. He was a semi-portable steam engine: a round-bellied oven coupled to an upright, broad-shouldered engine. He exuded a heavy aroma of hot iron with a tart overtone of coal smoke that made her thighs tingle. And he was for sale. Although Anna came to the fair every day for a week to get to know him properly, she had really made up her mind on the first day. She could just about afford him. Anna announced to her parents that she intended to visit a friend and her husband in Berlin, and possibly find a suitor there. Her parents made no resistance, and Anna didn't tell them her stay would be indefinite. She rented a warehouse on Stahlwerkstrasse and moved her possessions there.

Arriving at the warehouse with Hercules, Anna was greeted by a confused gentleman and a miniature airship who already occupied the space. The gentleman introduced himself as Dr. Hiller and wouldn't meet her gaze but showed her a document. They seemed to have identical leases for the warehouse on Stahlwerkstrasse. Anna and Franz visited the landlord's office, where a small seborrhoeic woman regretted the mix-up. Sadly, it was too late to save the situation, as all warehouses were now occupied. She was, however, convinced that Dr. Hiller and Fräulein Goldberg could solve the situation between them. As long as the rent was paid every month, it wasn't very important how. They would even get a discount for their troubles. With that, she thanked them for their visit and asked them to leave.

"I can't have people burning things in the warehouse," said Franz once they exited onto the street. "The airship is very flammable."

"What does Dr. Hiller do with it?" said Anna.

"I don't think that is of Fräulein Goldberg's concern," said Franz. "What is Fräulein Goldberg going to power with her steam engine?"

Anna stared at him with a blush that started at her neck and crept up her cheeks. "His name is Hercules," she said quietly.

Franz stopped and looked at her. "Oh," he said after a moment, and his eyes softened. "I apologize. I think we share the same fate."

Returning to the warehouse, Franz led Anna to the airship moored in the far end of the room. "This is Beatrice," he said, and laid a possessive hand on Beatrice's gondola.

Anna greeted Beatrice with a nod. "My congratulations," she told Franz. "She is very beautiful."

They agreed on sharing the warehouse, with a partition in the middle. Anna brought a simple woodstove. After she pointed out that he, too, would need to cook for himself, Franz allowed her to install it in an alcove in the middle of the far wall of the warehouse, as far away from Beatrice as possible. The alcove became a shared kitchen and sitting room. It even took on a cozy air.

Anna was constantly at work shoveling coal into Hercules's gaping maw and topping up water for the steam. At night, she would get up every other hour to feed him. Franz, who left for the clinic each morning, imagined she would do the same in the daytime as well, as she was often busy shoveling coal no matter what time of day he came home. Other than that, she mostly seemed to be busy reading technical manuals and papers. She had brought an entire bookcase full of them.

Beatrice remained cold and distant, no matter how Franz tried to warm their relationship. He was meticulous in his care for her. He read newspapers to her daily; he made love to her with great care. Nothing seemed to get her attention. Should he have tried harder to win the first Beatrice? Should he have pursued her more? Why hadn't he? And the question that plagued him the most—had Beatrice loved him as violently as he loved her? One night, he told Anna the whole story over a shared supper.

"I'll never find out," he said. "Did she really love me? Would I have loved her at all, once I got to know her? Perhaps it was just a dream. She might be nothing like I thought she was."

Anna shook her head, smoothing the pages of the journal she was reading. "I learned something from falling in love with that Koenig & Bauer. Infatuation is worth nothing. It has nothing to do with the real world." She nodded at the steam engine looming in the corner by her bed. "Me and Hercules, we have an understanding. We take care of each other. It's a better kind of love, I think."

"This Beatrice might come to love me, don't you think?" Franz said.

"She might," said Anna. "And you have her right here. That's more than you can say about the other."

Anna's relationship to Hercules did seem much happier in comparison, especially when her belly started to swell. The pregnancy was uncomplicated, even though Anna sometimes complained of strange sensations in her stomach. When Franz laid an ear to her belly, he could hear clicking and whirring sounds in there.

"What will you do when it's time?" he asked.

"I can't go to the hospital," said Anna. "They'll take the child from me. You'll have to help me."

Franz couldn't say no. He stole what he might need from the clinic, a little at a time: suture, tongs, morphine, iodine solution. He had only delivered babies twice, and never on his own, but he didn't tell Anna this.

. . .

Even when she had contractions, Anna kept feeding Hercules. She wouldn't let Franz do it. She didn't stop until she went into labor. The delivery was a quick process. The child was small but healthy, its pistons well integrated with the flesh. But once the placenta had emerged, the bleeding wouldn't stop. Anna bled out in the warehouse, the child on her belly.

"Put me in Hercules," were her last faint words. "I want to be inside him."

Franz did as she asked. First he gently washed the child, wrapped it in clean linen, and put it in a basket next to Anna's bed. Then he turned to Anna where she lay on the bed. He wiped the blood off her body with a wet cloth and folded a clean sheet around her. He lifted her off the bed with some difficulty and carried her over to where Hercules waited. She fit in the oven perfectly.

"That's the last you'll get," he told Hercules. "I'm not going to feed you."

The steam engine seemed to glare at Franz from its corner. The oven hatch glowed with the heat from Anna's body. Franz turned his back on it and picked the baby up, cradling it in his arms. It opened its mouth and cried with a whistling noise. Franz walked over to his side of the warehouse, holding the baby up in front of his airship.

"We're foster parents now, Beatrice," he said.

For the first time he could sense a reaction from her. It felt like approval, but it wasn't directed at him.

The child was a girl. Franz named her Josephine. He tried to feed her cow's milk at first, but she spit it out, hissing. She steadily lost weight, her pistons squealing and rasping, until Franz in desperation dissolved some coal in water, dipped the end of a rag in it, and stuck it in her mouth. When Josephine immediately sucked the rag dry, Franz understood what kind of care his foster daughter needed. He took the box of maintenance tools Anna had kept for Hercules and greased Josephine's pistons carefully with good oil. He fed her a steady diet of coal water, gradually increasing the coal until it was a thick paste. When she had enough teeth, he gave her small bits of coal to gnaw on. The girl didn't need diapers, as she didn't produce any waste; she seemed to spend whatever she ate as body heat. If he fed her too much, she became unbearably hot to the touch, her pistons burning his hands. These peculiarities aside, she behaved much like a normal baby.

Franz wrote a letter of resignation to the clinic. He sold Hercules to a factory, and Anna's furniture to an auction house. The money would be enough for rent and food for a long time to come, if he spent it wisely. He would at least be able to take care of his airship and his foster daughter. Whenever he had to leave their home, he put the baby in Beatrice's gondola. When he came back, the baby was always in a good humor, comfortably cradled in the otherwise hard seat, cooing and playing with dials or tubes that had somehow come loose from the console. When Josephine was old enough not to need constant feeding, he found work at another clinic. Josephine seemed content to spend her days in the gondola. Beatrice radiated affection whenever the girl was near.

The catastrophe came when Josephine was four years old. The little girl didn't have vocal cords, but instead a set of minuscule pipes arrayed in her larynx. She whistled and tweeted until her fourth birthday, when she suddenly started modulating the noise into speech. It was early morning. They had just finished breakfast. Josephine was sitting on the table, Franz lubricating the pistons in her arms. Josephine opened her mouth and said in a high, fluting voice:

"Father, her name isn't Beatrice."

"Is that so," said Franz, dripping oil on her finger joints.

"She says so every time you call her Beatrice. 'That's not my name,' she says."

Franz blinked. "Do you understand everything she says?"

"Her name isn't Beatrice," Josephine repeated. "It's something else. And she wants to say some things to you."

Josephine sat with her legs dangling from the gondola, warbling the airship's thoughts without seeming to grasp their meaning. Franz was informed of the following: The airship's name wasn't Beatrice. It was something entirely different. She had lived as a slave under Franz, and he had raped her while pretending she was someone else. She hated him.

"That can't be right," said Franz. "We worked on this marriage together. She was the one who wouldn't make an effort."

"She says, 'I had no choice,'" said Josephine. "She says, 'You're holding me captive.'"

Franz felt his throat constrict. "I certainly am not," he said. "I've worked so hard." He shoved his hands in his pockets to stop them from trembling. "I've worked so hard," he repeated.

"She wants to fly," said Josephine.

Franz opened the great double doors to the warehouse and slowly towed Beatrice outside. He knew what was going to happen. That Josephine was going to climb into the gondola while he was busy sorting out the tethers. That Beatrice II would tear free of her moorings and swiftly rise up into the sky, drifting east. That she would be gone in a matter of minutes, leaving him alone on the ground.

He sorted out the tethers. Meanwhile, Josephine climbed into the gondola. Beatrice II suddenly pulled at the moorings, which snapped, and she ascended without a sound. Franz stood outside the warehouse, watching the sky, until night fell.

Some Letters for Ove Lindström

HI, DAD.

It's Saturday and it's been thirty-six days since they found you. You lay in the apartment for three days before the neighbors called the police because the cat was howling. That was on a Friday. They said at the hospital it looked like a massive heart attack, probably quick. They asked if you and I were close. I said no: I couldn't cope with your drinking, broke off contact with you many years ago.

That same night I dreamed about Mom for the first time in many years. She was standing at the edge of the forest, her back turned. Her dark hair tumbled in tangles down her back. The hem of her red dress dragged at the ground. I was sitting in the sandbox. I couldn't move. She walked in among the trees and there was a tinkling sound on the air, like tiny bells.

I entered your apartment prepared for something like the last time I was there: floors covered by a thick layer of newspapers and milk cartons, piles of clothes, and dirty dishes on the furniture, and a layer of greasy filth over everything. Fruit flies in the kitchen. Maggots in the sink. The stench of rot and unwashed human.

But I opened the door to empty rooms and a smell of pine soap. Floors and surfaces were scrubbed clean, the kitchen immaculate. I couldn't see any bottles or beer cans. Did you quit drinking? When? There was no smell of smoke either. I wonder when you quit the cigarettes and when you decided to clean out the apartment. There were a couple of suitcases standing near the door.

I took care of the cat. I don't know what you named her, but I call her Squeak—she's thin as a pipe cleaner and meows like a squeaky toy. She's hungry and pissed off, but fine.

I called Björn and Maggie. Björn said he'd talked to you on Monday. You'd said you were getting your act together: going out to the old schoolhouse at Munsö to start over. It was going to be just like old times.

"Maybe he had a feeling something was about to happen," Björn said. "But on the other hand . . . I don't know. He would do that about once a year. He'd clean the flat and go to Munsö to start over, and then he'd come back a couple of weeks later and it'd be just like before."

"He never told me that," I said.

"Maybe he was afraid to. I know I was. I didn't tell you because I knew he'd just fall off the wagon again. Just as well you didn't hear about it."

I'm glad Björn didn't tell me.

These people came to the service: Björn and Maggie, Per-Arne, Eva and Ingeborg, Peter and Lena, Dolores, Magnus, Alice. I hadn't seen any of them except Björn and Maggie since I was maybe eighteen. They have changed. They're not just older. They came in expensive cars, with rounded bellies under designer shirts and dresses. They're not starving activists anymore. Björn and Maggie showed up in denim. That made me feel less abnormal. Maggie held my hand all through the service.

Most of them stayed for the funeral coffee. I had to answer questions about what I was up to these days. They offered apologies for not keeping in touch. It was because you had pushed them away. They hadn't been able to cope with it.

Then they talked about old times, telling the obligatory story about how it all started. How a surly farmer (you) was persuaded to rent out the old schoolhouse to a bunch of hairy communists from the city. How the surly farmer eventually joined them and grew a beard. All the parties, and the harvest festival, and the magazine they printed on a hand-cranked printing press in the cellar; and the first commune baby (me), tiny and fat and precocious, who could chant "U.S. out of Vietnam, Laos, and Cambodia!" by the age of two. We didn't mention Mom. Then it was over, everyone went home, and I don't expect I'll see any of them again except Björn and Maggie.

You'll be buried next to Sten and Alva, your parents that I know nothing about. You never told me anything about them, only that they were sickly and died early. It seems to be a family trait.

—Viveka

Hi, Dad.

I finished the paperwork last week. I figured I'm between jobs anyway, so I might as well go on a trip. I'm sitting at the kitchen table in the janitor's house at Munsö. That makes me the fourth generation to own the schoolhouse.

I brought Squeaky. She seems familiar with the place. She catches mice, crunching on them under the table. She's a tidy eater, leaving only the hearts. I find them here and there, lying on the floor like red raisins.

You must have been here in the spring. The hothouse is full of squash, tomatoes, beans, and pumpkins, ready for harvest. The pantry's full. There's even firewood, and it's clean. I found mint tea. It's the same sort you used to drink when I was little. These are the smells from when things were good—firewood, mint tea, and old house.

I used to sleep on the sofa bed in the kitchen, you in the bedroom. You were too tall for the sofa bed, you said, otherwise you'd let me have the bedroom. You were always a little hunched over, hitting your head on doorjambs and lamps. I can see you standing over the sofa bed, reaching out with a long hand to pull the covers all the way up to my chin. Snug like a dolma, you would say.

I'm sleeping in the bedroom tonight. I've grown too tall for the sofa bed.

If only you'd kept a journal. The only thing that tells me how much time you spent here are the newspapers by the stove. About once a year, for a few weeks at a time, just like Björn said. According to *Svenska Dagbladet* (which you insisted on reading despite calling it a bourgeoisie rag), the last time was in May.

I went over to the schoolhouse today. The front door had warped, and was difficult to get open. In the cloakroom I turned right and the long tables still stood there, and the benches, and the serving table at the back. The breeze blowing in from the open door stirred up dust in the air. The fly-papers spiraling down from the ceiling were black with little corpses. I went into the kitchen at the back: the old orange curtains still hanging in the windows, the massive rounded refrigerator graying in the corner. Through the kitchen into the common room with its brown corduroy couches and the IKEA bookshelves: dust and silence. The smell of wood and mold. Through the common room, full circle into the cloak-room. Up the steep stairs at the back of the cloakroom, with the rosette window halfway up. The attic with its bedrooms that used to be storage, like empty monk cells in a row. I remember everyone leaving: Lena packing the huge toy tur-tle, its plush skin worn through where I had sat on it every day. I cried when she stuffed it into a box.

The empty gravel driveway, the hothouse that slowly went to seed, the absence of voices, before you boarded up the school-house and janitor's house and packed our things into the car.

In the photos of you and Mom, you're so in love, so lost in her. One of the pictures is of the schoolhouse steps. She's standing with a hand on the rail, looking into the camera. She's wearing a knee-length black dress with a white yin-yang pattern, her belly big and round. You're wearing jeans and an orange shirt, one hand resting on her belly. Ignoring the photographer, you're looking sideways at Mom with a soft smile. She's so tall. You're not hunched over next to her. You smile like that in all the photos from then, Dad.

—Viveka

Hi Dad.

I got your bike out from the shed—you kept it in good shape—and went down to the old co-op for food. I used the forest path that goes past the lake. It took about half an hour when I was a kid, but this time I must have taken a wrong turn; here and there I couldn't recognize where I was. It took me an hour to get there. Things are supposed to feel much smaller when you visit places from your childhood. The old co-op was unrecognizable. They've renovated. Not that it helps. They don't know what tofu is.

This is my very first memory: it was August. I was three years old. Vladimir Vysotsky was rasping through the gramophone. The air smelled of damp wool and crayfish and toast. It was getting cold. You opened your cardigan so I could climb inside, and then buttoned it up again so that I sat there like a kangaroo pup, head sticking out, your beard tickling at my neck. When you sang along in the chorus, my whole back vibrated. Mom sat across the table. She was staring at us, her face very still.

Of course she refused to give birth in a hospital. Maggie has told me so many times. She gave birth in the janitor's house, assisted by one of the commune members (Annika?) who happened to be a certified midwife. It took eleven hours. I was healthy and weighed three and a half kilos. You didn't take me to the hospital. I wasn't to be registered, checked, or vaccinated. You wanted the authorities to stay out of our lives.

It'll be the twenty-fifth anniversary of her disappearance, soon.

"Do you know what your father used to say," Maggie said once. "He used to say that your mother just came out of the forest one day."

I'm having tea on the veranda. It's still warm out. A few more weeks and the forest will be full of mushrooms. And all the vegetables in the hothouse, I wonder if I could learn to can them so they don't spoil. Weren't Lena and Peter fanatics about that stuff?

The cell phone rang for the first time since I arrived here. It was my caseworker at the unemployment center who wanted to know why I didn't show up for our meeting yesterday. It had completely slipped my mind. Caseworker wants me to report for inspection immediately. If I don't provide a list of all the jobs I've applied for this month, my benefits will be cut off. I figure that's about to happen anyway, so what difference does it make? I'll be cut off, and then I'll have to apply for welfare, and they'll tell me I can't have any because I own property. Then I'll either have to sell this place or tell the welfare people to sod off. In which case I'll settle out here and live on mushrooms and canned vegetables. I wonder how long I could do that. I wonder how long it would take before anyone except my caseworker missed me.

—Viveka

Hi Dad.

I've been weeding in the hothouse. Some of the plants died during the summer, others are growing wild. It's not much of a hothouse, what with the hole in the roof. The vegetables going nuts are the ones that got rain on them. I don't think I could survive on them if I lose my benefits.

This is my second memory: I know now that it's about a week after the crayfish party. I was sitting in the sandbox outside the house. The sand was cold and damp under the dry top layer. I had taken my shoes off, digging into the chill with my toes. Mom kissed my forehead and then she walked away. She was wearing the red dress. She was barefoot. Mom walked in amongst the trees and there was a tinkling sound on the air, like tiny bells.

You came back from the store to find me howling in the sandbox. You put off calling the police until the next day. You tried to report her missing, but were told she didn't exist. She wasn't in the national registry.

Of course, neither was I, which they found out. I was registered and received a personal identity number and the mandatory vaccinations.

And that was that. Mom didn't come back.

You did what a dad is supposed to do. You made sure I went to school; you cooked dinner; we watched television together; you helped me with homework. I was never yelled at. You were never mean. When you started drinking, it was quietly, in the armchair by the television. You'd get distant and fall asleep at odd times. I learned to make myself dinner.

I feel almost jet-lagged. The sun is so low in the sky. The sunset just goes on and on.

—Viveka

Hi Dad.

I thought you might want to know what I was doing while you were getting drunk. Once we'd moved into the two-roomer in Hökarängen I was over at Maggie and Björn's place most of the time. You didn't want to see them. You were at work, or you were watching television at home, drinking. One evening I was in Maggie and Björn's kitchen—we had just finished dinner—and I asked Maggie about you and Mom.

"Actually I don't remember how it was," said Maggie. "She

didn't arrive with any of the others—it was me, Björn, and Peter from the Jester commune, Eva and Ingeborg from Nyköping; Per-Arne was from Norrköping, he was Ingeborg's friend from FNL . . . but your mother, I don't remember how she ended up there. But she was there from the start, that she was. A very private person. She and your father were a good match that way, I suppose. They liked keeping to themselves."

"How do you mean, private," I said.

"She never talked about herself. I mean, she didn't talk about personal stuff, or offer opinions. I never found out what she thought about anything, not in all the years she was there. We thought she was a bit touched, or she'd been through something difficult, so we didn't make a big deal of it. And then there was that bit about her not being in the national registry. Maybe her identity was protected. Maybe she'd run away from an abusive husband. That's what I think. But why she left you and your dad . . ." Maggie patted my cheek. She put an arm around me. "That was a shitty thing to do," she said. "If I'd had a child like you, I wouldn't have left you for a second."

I sat quietly inhaling Maggie's scent, a mix of softener, cigarettes, and warm skin.

"Do you know what your father used to say," Maggie said. "He used to say that your mother just came out of the forest one day."

I tried to call Maggie just now, but for some reason I have no reception. It would be good to hear her voice.

—Viveka

Hi Dad.

When I was little, I could sit for hours looking out the window. It could be because of a certain kind of music, or because it was dusk, or a certain slant of the light. There was a sensation in my chest, a churning. I couldn't put words to it then. But it was a knowledge that there was something out there. That there was a hole in the world. And a longing to go there. I still have that longing, but it doesn't overwhelm me like it used to. Until now. There's something about the light here that makes the longing bloom.

I'm thinking about the last time I saw you alive. It was four years after I had left home. You called sometimes when you were drunk, saying everything would get better. In the end I changed my phone number.

Then it was your fiftieth birthday, and I thought I'd give it a chance. I knocked on your door at about seven in the evening. There was no reply, but the door wasn't locked. In there was the wino den. Something under the garbage rustled in a corner.

You were on the couch, watching TV. You looked up when I came in, old milk cartons crunching under my boots.

"I was at the schoolhouse, you know?" you said. "I did clean up in here. And I went to the schoolhouse. I waited for her to come back. But she didn't."

You started to weep. It was a wet and forlorn sobbing. I turned around and left. It would be six years until I saw you next.

Inside the schoolhouse, I pretend that no time has passed. Closing my eyes, I can hear the others. The rhythmic thud of kneading dough. Something being chopped on a cutting board. Someone strumming a guitar and humming the melody. Footsteps on the stairs. The smell of baking bread and tea and onions frying in butter. A hand caressing my cheek in passing. I pretend that it's dinnertime. We sing together, and then we fill our plates. I can sit in anyone's lap. I lean against a shoulder. When I've fallen asleep, they carry me to the brown corduroy couch in the corner of the dining hall and put a blanket over me. The corduroy is rough against my face. The buzz of voices rising and falling.

Dad

The sun didn't rise today. I can only see it as a glow on the horizon. I was in the kitchen when the noise came. I could hear it all the way inside. I went out onto the veranda. It was the sound of little bells. I hadn't heard it since the day Mom left.

I tried to call Maggie. No reception. So I'm sitting here on the steps. The sound of bells still hangs in the air. And the twilight just lingering there, that won't go toward night or day.

Dad, I think Mom is coming soon.

Miss Nyberg and I

IT BEGAN WITH A FAINT, SCRAPING NOISE on the balcony.

That's how I think things began for you, anyway. For me, it started one late night in your room. It's many years ago now, back when we were young. I was reminded of it because you mentioned that you'd planted sequoia. You did that when I rented a room in your apartment, and we snuck a plant into the flower bed outside the house, and somehow it managed to take root in the stern Swedish soil. After twenty years, the tree had managed to dig its roots all the way down into the laundry room of an adjacent house.

It's a Sunday in late February. We're on the big red plush sofa that I love, but is so damned hard to get out of. You've made a tart apple crumble, almost no sugar, but extra crumble. We cover it in lakes of custard and talk about our aches and pains: my new hip joint, your sciatica, my novel, your exhibition. And about the sequoia on the balcony, about to slowly wake from winter sleep. And I realize I've never told you the story about Brown.

It was summer. You worked nights as an illustrator at a tabloid. We shared a landline phone. I woke up at dawn because I thought I heard it ringing. The phone was quiet when I opened the door to your room. But there was someone in the gloom, sitting on the wooden chest you used for a coffee table. It was a small, gnarled shape with a faint glimmer of eyes. In my half-sleeping state, it didn't seem that odd.

When I woke up again, I wasn't sure if I had actually been in your room that night. But the image of the creature on the coffee table stuck in my head. It turned into a short story that was never finished—I had trouble with the ending. It also felt a bit weird that a friend of mine was the main character. I could have changed her name, but it wouldn't have been the same thing. I mean, the story was about *you*.

This also has to do with your penchant for strange plants. You weren't very interested in growing boring, ordinary flowers. Possibly sweet pea, because they were so pretty. Other than that, though, you preferred to order the most bizarre stuff you could find in the seed catalog, some of it on general principle:

"Angel trumpets! They ought to be illegal. I'll have to grow those."

You liked mandrake and deadly nightshade for the same reason. (This was the year your project was to fill the balcony with poisonous plants.) And then there were the surprise bags you ordered and opened with glee: mixed, unlabeled seeds that could sprout into anything.

· · ·

So when all this happened, I reckon it was late March, when the snowdrops start to wilt and crocus stick their buds out of the ground, when gravel and salt still litter the streets. It was dusk, and the first blackbird warbled in the pine next to the building. You opened the balcony door to let some air in, and you wouldn't have looked down at the sleeping flowerpots if it weren't for that scraping noise. There was a very small creature between two of the pots, trying to escape attention by standing very still. It was shivering from the cold.

It was knotted and dusted with soil, knees and elbows worn shiny. It was perhaps four inches tall. It made no resistance as you bent down and picked it up, lifted it into the kitchen and put it down on the table. You looked at each other for a while. Then you said:

"Did I grow you?"

It nodded in reply.

It was seemingly a sexless creature, but thin and crooked as it was, it looked like an old man. You simply named him Brown, and you made a bed for him in a blue flowerpot in the kitchen window.

Brown either couldn't speak or chose not to. He was a quiet presence who seemed content to sit among the plants in the kitchen window. He would climb down to sit on the kitchen table when you ate. He disappeared under the dirt in the blue flowerpot whenever you had visitors.

I wrote some stuff about how Brown seemed to have a personal relationship with each of the plants in your flat and on the balcony. He made his rounds every day, patting stems and leaves, sometimes just sitting still among the roots. In spring, little buds sprung out on his shoulders and elbows that bloomed in time for midsummer. During winter, he hibernated in the flowerpot.

I wrote about when you moved from Hökarängen to another suburb west of Stockholm, and how Brown almost died because the transition was so difficult. And there the text ended. I didn't know what to write, how to make the story come together. Where would it end? Would Brown stay with you the rest of your life? Would he ever be discovered by someone else? If someone moved in with you, how would he be able to stay hidden? To answer all these questions I would have to invent your future life. Your career. Your travels. A partner, maybe more. This is easy enough with a fictitious person, but you were very real, and my friend. Who was I to decide what you would do for a living, what kind of people you would come to love? I ended up being so afraid of doing something wrong, as if I were about to force you into a literary arranged marriage, that I stopped writing in the middle of the move from Hökarängen and Brown's imminent death.

We know now how things ended up, of course. Alice's gentle siesta snores reach out into the living room. Your paintings cover the walls. Brown's presence, I say, must have gone unnoticed, or he's become a family secret. Of course, I didn't think you'd ever share your life with someone who couldn't handle the existence of someone like Brown.

You're still listening, uncharacteristically quiet. When I say these last things, you smile at me—that very Finnish smile that makes you look so much like your mother, slanted eyes almost disappearing into the folds of your face. You chortle at me.

"I know, I know," I say. "But what the hell was I supposed to do? You of all people know I can't stop making things up."

You burst into laughter. You stand up and walk over to the window, where you lift an upside-down flowerpot. A tiny, gnarled creature lies curled up on a folded woolen sock. It seems to be asleep. I can see its tiny rib cage moving.

"Brown," you say. "What a name."

Rebecka

THE OUTLINE of Rebecka's body is light against the scorched wall, arms outstretched as if to embrace someone. The floor is littered with white ashes. Everything else in the room looks like it did before. A kitchen table with a blue tablecloth, a kitchenette stacked with dirty dishes. A wrought iron bed, which I am strapped to.

I ended up here because I was Rebecka's only friend. As such, I used to clean up after her half-hearted suicide attempts: blood from shallow wrist cuts; regurgitated benzos and vodka; torn-out overhead light sockets and doorjambs that wouldn't hold her weight. She would call me in the wee hours of the morning: *Get over here, help me, I tried again, I screwed up* ... and I would go over there to nurse her and hug her, again and again. What was I supposed to do? I wanted to tell her to do something radical—jump from the West Bridge, throw herself in front of a train—just to get it over with. But I didn't have the heart. I don't know why I remained her friend. It's not like I got anything out of it. It was the worst kind of friendship, held together by pity.

I remember the phone conversation we had the day before her first suicide attempt. It was a slushy Saturday in March. I was in my pajamas on the sofa, watching two sparrows fight over a lump of tallow that hung from the balcony rail. We were talking about something inconsequential, clothes and sizes I think, when she suddenly changed the subject.

"The Lord," Rebecka said over the phone.

"Hallowed be His name," I said reflexively.

"Sure. The Lord," she said. "He punishes people, right?"

"Is that a trick question?" I said.

She was quiet for a moment. Then: "I did something."

"What?"

"I went to the Katarina Church and spit in the baptismal font."

"You did what?" I must have shouted; the birds took off.

"Spit in the baptismal font. I thought that might get His attention."

"Rebecka, that's insane. People have been fried on the spot for doing stuff like that."

"Yeah, that was sort of the point, wasn't it?"

"So what happened?"

"Well, He showed up."

I waited for her to say she was just pulling my leg, but she said nothing, just breathed down the line. "He showed up? How?"

"Uh," she said, "it was really bright. I had to cover my eyes."

I looked outside. Melting icicles on the windows and rain

gutters that glittered in sunlight unbearably bright after the foggy Stockholm winter. "Uh-huh," I said.

"But He said He was okay about the font," she continued. "He said that some people have to be allowed more mistakes than others. That they're damaged and don't understand."

"Did you get a chance to ask Him about the other stuff?"

"No. He left after that. I'll have to come up with something else."

"Rebecka," I said, "you can't make Him change His mind."

"I just don't want to feel like shit. Is that too much to ask?"

"We can't expect Him to take care of everything," I said. "After all, we had to take care of ourselves before He came back."

"But there were psychologists then," she said.

"Yes."

"And there aren't anymore."

"No, I guess not."

"Because He cures everyone and . . . how was it . . . 'lifts the darkness in every soul.' Except me. So what am I going to do?"

"I don't know. Maybe it's a task you have. A test."

"I already went through my damned test. I can't deal with all this crap." She hung up.

The string of attempts with pills, razor blades, and ropes started after that. She would call me after every attempt. I took her to the hospital the first few times. After making sure she didn't have any life-threatening injuries (and she never did), they sent her home with a priest in tow. Eventually, Rebecka wouldn't call me until a day or so after she'd done something. Then I'd visit to clean up the mess while she hid in her bed.

The Lord tells us we must have patience with our fellow men, especially those who are being tested. Rebecka was being tested. Around the time when I had just met her, she had been raped and tortured by her husband, rest his soul. She had never recovered.

"People who hurt others are the ones with the best imagination," Rebecka said.

We were walking along the quay from Old Town to Slussen, watching the commuter boats trudge across Lake Mälaren. It was November. There were no tourists waiting for the boats this time of year, just some pensioners and a kindergarten group in bright snowsuits. I didn't mind the cold, but Rebecka was bundled up. We each had a cup of coffee, Rebecka occasionally pulling down her scarf from her face to take a sip. I couldn't help but look at her scarred lips as she did so.

"I don't follow," I said.

"Would you get the idea to cut a pregnant woman open with a bread knife and take the baby out?" She was talking through her scarf again, voice muffled.

I shuddered. "Of course not."

"Or poke someone's eyes out with a paper clip?"

"Come off it."

"Three days, Sara."

Of course. This was what she was on about. Karl.

"He used everything he could get his hands on."

"I know, Becks. You've told me everything."

She went on as if I hadn't said anything. "You couldn't imagine the things he came up with, not in your worst nightmares. Get it? And you know something else?"

"What?" I said, although I knew what she was going to say.

"How could He let it go on for three days before He decided to do something about it?"

"He did deal with him," I said, as I usually did.

"Yeah, after three days. Why did He wait so long?"

"I don't know."

We were quiet for a while, sipping coffee.

"And I'm still here," Rebecka said. "It's like I'm being punished too."

"I don't think you are," I said. "You're not being punished. He doesn't do that. Like I said before, maybe it's a test."

We went through the motions like that, until I said I had to go home and dropped her off at Slussen, where she would take the subway.

She didn't take the subway. She tried to throw herself in front of it. It was in all the morning papers: Rebecka jumped from the end of the platform, so that the train would hit her at full speed. The driver later told reporters that he'd had a sudden impulse to brake before he was supposed to. The train had stopped a meter from where Rebecka was lying on the tracks.

"Maybe now you'll believe me when I tell you," she said across the kitchen table the following day. "Listen, I'm ashamed for all the times you've had to come and clean me up."

"It's all right," I said.

"No, it's not. I know you think I'm a coward who's afraid to really go ahead and kill myself. I know you wish I could make up my mind and either die or start living again."

I couldn't meet her eyes then.

"It's always been for real," she said. "It really has. I can't sleep through a single night without waking up because Karl is there. He's standing at the foot of the bed, and I know he's about to do all those things to me. I want it to stop. I want to sleep." She looked at me. "Every time I went for my arms with the razor they stopped bleeding. Every time I took pills and alcohol I started throwing up. I never once stuck my fingers down my throat. I promise. I just started throwing up. And if I didn't, absolutely nothing would happen even though I should be passing out."

"So what are you saying?" I said.

"It's getting worse. I don't even get injured anymore. I swallowed a bottle of sleeping pills yesterday, you know?"

"And . . . ?"

"They came out the other end this morning. Whole. The Lord is fucking with me."

"Don't swear," I said.

"I'm telling you. The Lord is fucking with me. I hate Him. He won't take the nightmares away. Or the scars, all the scars. But He won't let me kill myself, either. It's like He wants me to suffer."

"Rebecka, we've been through this one before."

"Would you stop taking His side all the time?" she shouted. "I'm your best friend!"

"Rebecka," I said.

"I know what you're going to say. He's not my nanny."

"That wasn't what I was going to say."

"If He thinks I'm supposed to deal with this myself, He could have just not come back in the first place. That way I would have known what to do. But now, this is the way things are. And I really don't know what I'm supposed to do."

"Me neither," I said.

. . .

The next time Rebecka called it was early morning.

"You have to come over," she said. "We have to talk."

I took the bike over to her apartment, expecting to see another scene of a failed suicide attempt. Her face was pale under the scarring when she opened the door.

"Hi," she said.

"Hi," I said. "I've taken the day off."

She let me in. There wasn't anything on her or in the apartment to indicate she had done anything to herself, just the usual mess. I sat down by the kitchen table while she poured tea. The blue tablecloth was crusted with cup rings. I traced them with a finger.

"You had me worried," I said. "What's going on?"

"I've realized what I have to do." She put a steaming cup in front of me and sat down in the opposite chair. A smoky Lapsang smell wafted up from the cup. Rebecka rested her elbows on the table and leaned toward me.

"I'm serious about not coping anymore," she said. Her tone was matter-of-fact. "I want to die, Sara."

"I don't want you to," I said.

"Are you sure?"

"I really don't want you to."

"Well, it's not for you to decide, anyway." She took a sip from her cup. I didn't know what to say, so I drank my tea. It was sweetened with too much honey.

"I suppose you're going to tell me," I said eventually.

"The Lord isn't going to do anything," Rebecka said. "I know that now."

There were white dregs at the bottom of my cup.

"Rebecka, what did you put in my tea?" I said.

Her face was set, almost serene. "I'm going to make Him listen," she replied. "I'm going to do something he can't ignore."

I was naked when I woke up in her bed. My wrists and ankles were tied to the bedposts. Rebecka was sitting on a chair beside me, a toolbox at her feet.

"I love you," I said.

"I know," she said.

Herr Cederberg

HERR CEDERBERG preferred leaving the office to have lunch outside. He would sit on a bench next to the fountain on Mariatorget, reading the newspaper with a sandwich or two, especially now that the weather was nice. It was June, and the flower beds were full of giddy insects that every now and then buzzed over to Herr Cederberg to make sure he wasn't a flower. Other office workers populated the adjacent benches with their lunch boxes, and some even stretched out on the lawns, drinking the first summer sun like pale lizards.

Herr Cederberg was vaguely reading an article on the national economy when feet crunched by on the gravel, and a girl's voice mumbled, ". . . like a bumblebee."

Another voice tittered. He didn't have to look up to know they were talking about him. He was already very aware of his swelling thighs and bulging stomach and that his feet were not quite touching the ground. The most common simile was pig, followed by panda, koala, and bumblebee, in no particular order. Herr Cederberg looked up from his newspaper. Two rosy and adolescent faces quickly looked away and leaned toward each other. The one who had giggled continued:

"Oh, I love bumblebees, they're so neat. You know how the laws of nature say they shouldn't be able to fly, right, but they fly anyway?"

"Yeah, but how?" asked the first girl.

"Because they don't know they're not supposed to!"

The girls burst into shrill laughter. Herr Cederberg couldn't summon the energy to say anything. They had no idea of their own idiocy and wouldn't for years to come, if ever. He looked at the fat little insects bumping around in the tulips, their wings, if one could see them in slow motion, oscillating in a beautiful figure-eight pattern. He imagined himself fluttering his arms in the same fashion, slowly ascending into the sky.

Herr Cederberg had long ago converted his garage into a workshop. His first passion had been for model planes, but the last few years he had been experimenting with different types of kites. His finest work to date, a Balinese dragon, covered the ceiling in bright red and gold.

He surveyed the little space. There was plenty of material to work with. He rolled up his shirtsleeves, took off his jacket, and started sketching a framework.

Herr Cederberg finished the machine on an early morning in the second week of August. At first glance, it resembled a stubby-winged canoe on wheels. The cockpit had a corduroy seat with a safety belt. A pair of bicycle pedals stuck out of the floor. It had felt a little banal to use pedals to power the wings, but they turned out to be the perfect method for creating the oscillating pattern he wanted. The chassis was covered with a layer of oilcloth, painted with black and yellow stripes. Herr Cederberg realized he hadn't given the craft a name.

After a long blank moment, he patted the chassis and said, "Bumblebee." He blushed at his own lack of imagination.

It was time to go. He folded the wings along the sides and pushed *Bumblebee* out of the garage, toward the forest.

Herr Cederberg stood sweaty and winded on the edge of a cliff in the forest outside the suburb. Far below lay the lake and the dark green sea of the pine forest. Next to him, the craft sat with its wings extended and a couple of wedges under its wheels to keep it from running off the edge. Herr Cederberg put his goggles on and crawled into the cockpit. He fastened his seat belt and waited.

The morning wind was too gentle, but after midday it finally picked up speed. A low-pressure front was heading in, and the chubby cumuli fused and inflated as they wandered the horizon. When the draft finally arrived, Herr Cederberg tore the wedges off and cheered quietly as the craft rolled forward, lifted its nose, and slid out over the edge. He pedaled as fast as his legs could manage. The wings were sluggish at first but picked up speed, and when an updraft shot up along the cliff, *Bumblebee* really took off. The air rushing by made Herr Cederberg's cheeks flutter. He rose higher and higher at a steep and determined angle.

The low-pressure front came in straight ahead. The

cumuli had gained height and metamorphosed into an enormous cumulonimbus, an anvil-shaped mass that stretched up into the higher layers of the atmosphere. Herr Cederberg looked down at the ground. He looked up at the cloud. Then he smiled and pedaled faster.

At first, the suction of the cumulonimbus felt like a faint increase in wind. Then suddenly, it was as if someone had grabbed the craft, as the cloud greedily started sucking in all air in its vicinity. Herr Cederberg saw the dark belly of the cloud stretch out like a bruised ceiling. The wind howled in his ears. The cloud ceiling soon filled his entire field of vision.

The forward motion turned into a violent updraft, and the air darkened around him. *Bumblebee* began to shudder and shake. A wing abruptly tore away and pulled half of the oilcloth with it. Herr Cederberg clung to the edges of the cockpit with whitening knuckles as the cold and dark closed in around him. Ice crystals flocked to his eyelashes and mustache. The other wing fell away into the fog. Herr Cederberg unfastened his safety belt and kicked away from the cockpit. The craft's remains disappeared under him. The fog brightened slightly. He closed his eyes.

Sometime later, the light became almost unbearably bright, and the wind quieted down. Herr Cederberg opened his eyes again. He was floating just above the top of the cumulonimbus cloud. Above him, a hard little sun shone in a sky colored dark violet. Little cirrus clouds powdered the stratosphere. White hills billowed away in all directions. The cold was deep and quiet. Herr Cederberg oscillated his arms, like a bumblebee.

Who Is Arvid Pekon?

DESPITE THE WELL-KNOWN FACT that it's the
worst time possible, everyone who needs to speak to a governmental agency calls on Monday morning. This Monday
was no exception. The tiny office was buzzing with activity,
the three operators on the day shift bent over their consoles
in front of the ancient switchboard.

On Arvid Pekon's console, Subject 1297's light was blinking. He adjusted his headset, plugged the end of the cord into
the jack by the lamp, and said in a mild voice:

"Operator."

"Eva Idegård, please," said Subject 1297 at the other end.

"One moment." Arvid flicked the mute switch and fed the
name into the little computer terminal under the wall of
lamps and jacks. Subject 1297 was named Samuelsson, Per.
Idegård, Eva was Samuelsson's caseworker at the unemployment insurance office. He read the basic information (*1297
unemployed for seven months*), listened to the voice sample,
and flicked the mute switch again.

"Gothenburg unemployment insurance office, Eva Idegård," Arvid said in a slightly hoarse alto voice.

"Hi, this is Per Samuelsson," said Per. "I wanted to check what's happening with my fee." He rattled off his personal registration number.

"Of course," said Arvid in Eva Idegård's voice.

He glanced at the information in the registry: *last conversation at 1:43 p.m., February 26: Subject's unemployment benefits were lowered and insurance fee raised because of reported illness but no doctor's certificate. (Subject did send a doctor's certificate—processed according to randomized destruction routine §2.4.a.)*

"You'll have to pay the maximum insurance fee, since we haven't received a doctor's certificate," said Arvid.

"I sent two of them in the original," said Per. "This isn't right."

"I suppose one could think that," said Arvid, "but the fact remains that we haven't received them."

"What the hell do you people do all day?" Per's voice was noticeably raised.

"You have a responsibility to keep us informed and send the right information to the unemployment benefit fund, Per," Arvid said in a soft voice.

"Bitch. Hag," Per said, and hung up.

Arvid removed his headset, massaged the sore spot it left above his right ear. He wrote in the log: *2:07 p.m., March 15: Have explained the raised fee.*

"Coffee break?" said Cornelia from the terminal to his right.

The light by Subject 3426 was blinking when Arvid sat down again.

"Operator," said Arvid, calling the details up on his screen. There was no information except for a surname: Sycorax, Miss. He hadn't seen this subject before.

"Hello?" said a voice. It was thin and flat.

"Yes, hello."

"I would like to be put through to my dead mother," said Miss Sycorax.

"Just a moment." Arvid muted the call. "Dead mother? How am I supposed to imitate her dead mother?" he said to his terminal. He peeked for the guidelines that should be popping up next to Miss Sycorax's name. There was nothing. Then he saw his hand rise up and flick the mute switch, and a sonorous voice burst out of his mouth. "Hello?"

"Mother, is that you?" said Miss Sycorax.

"Darling! Hello there. It's been a while, hasn't it?"

"Finding a good connection to Hell isn't easy, Mother."

Arvid fought to press his lips together. Instead they parted, and his mouth said: "It's lonely down here."

"Not much I can do about that, Mother," Miss Sycorax replied.

"Can't you come visit, just for once?" said Arvid, his voice dolorous. He desperately wanted to rip his headset off, but his hands lay like limp flippers in his lap.

"Well, if you're only going to be whiny about it, I think we can end this conversation," Miss Sycorax said tartly.

Arvid called her just that—tart—in her dead mother's voice. His ear clicked. Miss Sycorax had hung up. Arvid's hands were his own again. He took his headset off with shaky hands and looked around. At the next terminal, Cornelia was talking to Subject 2536 (*Persson, Mr., talking to an old friend from school in Vilhelmina*), twirling a lock of dark hair around her pencil as she spoke to the subject in an old man's voice. When she ended her call, Arvid stood up from his chair.

"I'll be leaving early," he said.

"Oh. Are you all right?" Cornelia asked, reverting to her melodic Finno-Swedish.

Arvid looked for any sign that she had overheard him talking in a dead person's voice, but thought he saw nothing but concern in her liquid brown eyes.

"Migraine, I think." Arvid took his coat from the back of the chair. "Migraine, I have a migraine."

"Go home and rest," said Cornelia. "It happened to me a lot when I was new. It'll get better, I promise." She turned back to her terminal to take a new call.

Arvid punched out and left the office. Outside, yellow afternoon light slanted through the street. As Arvid unlocked his bicycle, a woman in a phone booth next to the bicycle stand was arguing with someone. Arvid caught the words "unemployment" and "fee." He wondered briefly if that was Cornelia's call; she was unyielding in her caseworker personas.

Arvid did feel better the next day. By nine o'clock coffee, he felt more or less normal. As he entered the break room, he saw that Konrad, the senior operator, was carefully laying out pale cakes on a plate. Cornelia was stirring an enormous mug of coffee.

"*Kubbar!*" said Konrad. "I made them last night."

Arvid picked a cake from the plate and bit into it. It was dry and tasted of ammonia and bitter almonds. Cornelia was sniffing at hers.

"How are they?" Konrad asked. He was watching Arvid

eagerly. "I haven't made these for years. I was wondering if I got the proportions right."

"It's different," Arvid managed. He washed the cake down with some coffee.

"It tastes like cyanide shortbread," stated Cornelia. "Very Agatha Christie."

"Heh," said Konrad. He took a cake for himself and tasted it. "Your generation isn't used to ammonia cakes, I suppose."

Arvid had another one. The ammonia taste was strangely addictive.

"I have a question for you," Arvid said after a moment. "You've been here the longest. How are the subjects picked, really?"

Konrad shrugged and bit into his third *kubbe*. "No idea," he said. "I signed an NQ-NDA, just like you."

Arvid looked at Cornelia, who was chewing. She jerked a thumb at Konrad and nodded.

"So nobody knows?" said Arvid.

"The manager does, I expect," Konrad replied.

"But don't you ever wonder?"

"No Questions, No Disclosure, son. I'm not about to bite the hand that feeds me. Besides, all you need to know is in the work description. We take calls to governmental agencies . . ."

". . . and calls to persons the subjects don't know very well," Arvid filled in. "But——"

"And follow instructions. That's all there is to it. That's all you need to know. The manager relies on our discretion, Arvid. NQ-NDA."

Arvid sighed. "All right. What did you do before you got this job, anyway?"

"Stage actor," said Konrad. He picked a fourth *kubbe* from the plate. "Mhm?" he said, pointing at Arvid with the cake.

"Ventriloquist." Arvid nodded at Cornelia. "You?"

"Book audiotapes," said Cornelia.

Konrad swallowed. "See there, three crap jobs you can't make a living off of. Isn't it nice to be able to pay rent and eat good food?"

"I guess," said Arvid.

"You're new here. When you get over that starving artist thing, when you're my age, you'll agree that it's nice to be able to eat roast beef." Konrad pushed the plate toward Arvid. "Here, have another *kubbe*."

It was one week later, just after lunch, that Miss Sycorax's lamp started blinking again. Arvid hesitantly took the call.

"Hello," said the flat voice of Miss Sycorax.

"Where would you like to be connected?" said Arvid.

"I want to be connected to the Beetle King."

"I see," said Arvid, and muted Miss Sycorax. He cast a frantic glance at Cornelia, who was deeply involved in yet another call with Subject 9970, Anderberg. Mrs. Cornelia frowned and waved him off. He returned to Miss Sycorax.

"Miss, I'm afraid I really can't connect you to anyone by the name of . . . hello, my little pupa." A rustling voice forced its way out of his mouth midsentence.

"There you are," Miss Sycorax said. "I have a request."

"Anything for my little sugar lump," hummed Arvid.

"Aww, shucks," said Miss Sycorax.

"Your wish?"

"There are bugs crawling all over me."

"I know! Isn't it wonderful?" crowed Arvid.

"Hm. Yes, perhaps. In any case," she went on, "I'd like them to take some time off. I'm developing a rash."

"A rash, yes? An eczema."

"Yes. It's flaking a bit."

"And that isn't very pleasant."

"No. It itches."

"Well," said Arvid, "where should I send them off to, then?"

"Anywhere you like," said Miss Sycorax. "For example, I don't like the old woman in the corner store. Or the man who sells sticky window-pane-climbing dolls in Old Town."

"Aha."

"I don't like the switchboard operator, either."

"Let's say, then," said Arvid, "that we dismiss the little critters until you feel better."

"Good."

"And you let me know when you start feeling lonely again."

"Okay."

"Good-bye, honeycomb."

"Good-bye, Your Majesty."

When the Beetle King's voice had left him, Arvid sagged back in his chair.

"I might have gone mad," he told the terminal. He put his coat on and left the office.

When he came into the office the next day, Arvid found a stag beetle sitting on his terminal. It hissed angrily when he shooed it off, and crawled in under the desk where it refused to move. Shortly after morning coffee, a cockroach settled on his rules-and-regulations binder. Arvid left it alone.

Cornelia was more drastic about it. She had sat down in her chair to find the stuffing colonized by flour beetles. She was currently in the backyard, setting fire to the seat. The whole office smelled like insulin. Konrad sat at his terminal at the other end of the office, observing with great interest a dung beetle struggling with some cookie crumbs. No one was taking the incoming calls.

"Shouldn't we call pest control?" said Arvid.

"Can't get through," said Konrad, eyes on the beetle. "I heard something on the radio about a bug invasion in Old Town."

"Maybe it's the season for it," said Arvid.

"This dung beetle," said Konrad, "this beetle shouldn't be here at all. It's African. A very pretty specimen, actually." He gave it a piece of cookie to wrestle with.

Cornelia entered the office with a new chair. At the same time, the light by Miss Sycorax's number started blinking. Arvid considered not picking up. But Cornelia sat down and put her headset on, and Konrad tore himself away from the dung beetle, and there was no longer an excuse not to work. He pushed the button.

"Operator."

"Hello," said the flat voice.

"Yes, hello."

"I want to be put through to Arvid Pekon," said Miss Sycorax.

"Arvid Pekon," Arvid repeated. His finger flicked the mute switch up and down.

"Arvid," said his voice.

A slap woke him up. Cornelia's round eyes were staring worriedly into his. She turned her head to look over at Konrad's looming silhouette. They grabbed Arvid's arms and dragged him up into his chair.

"You had us worried there," said Cornelia.

"You fainted," Konrad explained.

"What happened?" asked Arvid. The buzzing in his head made it difficult to hear the other two. His face tingled.

"Oops. Head between your knees," said Konrad.

"What happened?" asked Arvid of the linoleum.

"You talked to 3426 for almost an hour and then you fell off your chair," said Cornelia.

"But I took the call just now."

"No, you've been going on for an hour."

"What did I talk about?"

Cornelia was silent for a moment. She was probably glaring at him. "You know we don't listen to each other's calls."

"Yes," mumbled Arvid to the floor.

A hand landed on his shoulder. "You should probably go home," said Konrad.

"I think I have to talk to the manager," said Arvid.

The door to the manager's office had an unmarked window of opaque glass. Arvid knocked on the glass. When there was no reply, he carefully pressed down the door handle and stepped inside. The room was smaller than he remembered it, but then again it was only his second time in here. There were no shelves or cabinets, just the enormous mahogany desk that covered most of the room. The desk was bare save for a telephone and a crossword puzzle magazine. Behind the desk, doing a crossword puzzle with a fountain pen, sat the manager in her powder-blue suit and immaculate gray curls. She looked up as Arvid opened the door and smiled, her cheeks drawing back in deep folds.

"Egyptian dung beetle, six letters?" said the manager.

Arvid opened his mouth.

"S-C-A-R-A-B," said the manager. "Thank you." She closed and folded the magazine, put it aside, and leaned back into her chair. She smiled again, with both rows of teeth.

Arvid waited.

"You have neglected to log three calls this month, Arvid," the manager said. "Subject 3426 at 2:35 p.m. on March 15; Subject 3426 at 1:10 p.m. on March 21; Subject 3426 at 4:56 p.m. on March 30. Why is this, Arvid?"

"I'm having a bit of trouble," Arvid said, and shifted his weight from side to side.

"Trouble." The manager was still smiling, cheeks folded back like accordions.

"I think I may be having a nervous breakdown."

"And that's why you haven't logged your calls."

"This is going to sound insane," said Arvid.

"Go on," said the manager.

Arvid took a deep breath. "Subject number 3426 . . ."

"Miss Sycorax," supplied the manager.

"Miss Sycorax," Arvid continued, "has been making some very strange calls."

"Many of our subjects do."

"Yes, but not like her. Something's off."

"I see."

"Eh, I don't know," he said. "Maybe I need some time off."

"If you think you're having a nervous breakdown, Arvid," said the manager, "I'll book an appointment with the company doctor and let him decide. We need to know if it's a workplace injury, you know. Oh, and do talk to Cornelia. She's the union representative."

"I will."

"All right, Arvid. Go on home. I'll have the doctor's office call you this afternoon." The manager smiled at him with both rows of teeth.

At the switchboard, Konrad and Cornelia were back at work. Cornelia was doing her best to ignore a little army of ants marching in a circle around her desk. Konrad and the dung beetle, on the other hand, seemed to have become fast friends. The dung beetle was rolling a sticky ball of masticated cookie crumbs.

Arvid sat down in his chair and stared at the terminal. After some hesitation, he put his headset on. Then he put a call through to Miss Sycorax.

"Hello," said Miss Sycorax after the third ring.

"Hello," echoed Arvid.

"Hello."

"This is the operator," Arvid managed.

"Oh."

Arvid took a deep breath. "Who is this Arvid Pekon you wanted to be put through to?"

At the other end of the line, Miss Sycorax burst into laughter. The sound made Arvid cower in his chair.

"It's a funny name," she said. "Pekon, it sounds like a fruit. Like plums or pears. Or like someone from China. Or like a dog breed."

"Who is Arvid Pekon?" Arvid repeated.

"There is no Arvid Pekon," Miss Sycorax replied.

"Yes there is!"

"No there isn't. I thought there was, but then I realized I was mistaken."

Arvid disconnected and tore his headset off.

"I'm right here!" he yelled at the cockroach on the in-box. "Look!" He banged his fist on the desk so hard that it tingled. "Would I be able to do that if I wasn't here?"

Something crackled. He looked down at his hand, which was lying in shards on the desk. The tingling sensation spread up his arm, which shuddered and then exploded in a cloud of dust.

"Where did Arvid go?" Cornelia asked Konrad a little while later.

"Who?" Konrad was looking at a ball of cookie crumbs on his desk, having no clear idea of how it got there. He popped it in his mouth.

Cornelia shook her head. "I don't know what I'm on about. Never mind."

"Coffee break?" said Konrad. "I've brought Finnish shortbread."

Brita's Holiday Village

5/29

THE CAB RIDE from Åre station to Aunt Brita's holiday village took about half an hour. I'm renting the cottage on the edge of the village that's reserved for relatives. The rest are closed for summer. Mom helped me make the reservation—Brita's her aunt, really, not mine, and they're pretty close. Yes, I'm thirty-two years old. Yes, I'm terrible at calling people I don't know.

I didn't bring a lot of stuff. Clothes and writing things, mostly. The cottage is a comforting old-fashioned red thing with white window frames, the interior more or less unchanged since the 1970s: lacquered pine, green felt wallpaper, woven tapestries decorated with little blobs of green glass. It smells stale in a cozy way. There's a desk by one of the windows in the living room, overlooking Kall Lake. No phone reception, no Internet. Brita wondered if I wanted a landline, but I said no. I said yes to the bicycle. The first thing I did was bike down to the ICA store I saw on the way here. I stocked up on pasta and tomatoes and beans. I found old-fashioned soft whey cheese, the kind that tastes like toffee. I'm eating it out of the box with a spoon.

"Holiday village" is a misleading expression; the village is really just twelve bungalows arranged in two concentric circles with a larger house—the assembly hall—in the middle. The dark paneling, angled roofs, and panoramic windows must have looked fresh and modern in the sixties, or whenever they were built. The wood is blackened now, and the windows somehow swallow the incoming light, creating caverns under the eaves. I'm a little relieved to be staying in the cottage.

Brita said that before she bought the holiday village, back when they were building it, the old man who owned the cottage refused to leave. When he finally died, the cottage was left standing for private use. It's much more cozy, anyway. I'd feel naked behind those panoramic windows.

5/30

I got up late and unpacked and sorted music. I've got a playlist with old punk and goth for the teenage project, an ambient playlist for the space project, and a list of cozy music, everything in order to feel at home and get into the mood and avoid writing. Did some cooking. Rode the bike around until I was tired. Found an old quarry. Tried to go for a swim in Kall Lake and cut my feet on the rocks. Bought goat whey curd. Finally, I couldn't avoid it anymore: writing.

So I have two stories I want to do something about. First there's the science fiction story about child workers in the engine room of a spaceship. It's a short story, really, but I'd like to expand it into a novel. I know you're not supposed to worry about form or length—it's a guaranteed way to jinx the whole thing—but I'd really like to. I like the characters and their intense relationships, like *Lord of the Flies* in space.

The other story is a pseudo-biographical thing about a teenager growing up in the Stockholm suburbia of the 1980s, during the heyday of Ultra, the tiny house turned punk headquarters. I suppose it's a cooler and bolder version of myself. Also, older. I was too young to ever hang out at Ultra. It had already burned down by the time I discovered punk. I used to go to Ultra's next iteration—Hunddagis, the club housed in an old day care center for dogs. I still remember the punk aroma: beer, cigarettes, cheap hair spray, and day-old sweat.

So, that's what I've been doing: writing down a bunch of teenage memories and transposing them onto a little older and bolder version of myself, and it's just slow and boring work. I had a go at the science fiction story instead, but it wouldn't happen. I ended up shutting everything down, realized it's now one o'clock in the morning (actually it's one thirty now), and I'm going to bed.

5/31

I took a walk through the village this morning. Things that look like white, plum-size pupae hang clustered under the eaves. They're warm to the touch. I should tell Brita—it's some kind of pest. Wasp nests?

Biked to the quarry after coffee, gathered some nice rocks— very pretty black granite. Went home, made pasta with chickpeas, tried to write. Writing about punks at Hunddagis doesn't feel the least bit fun or interesting. Mostly because

I've realized what a lame teenager I was. I was always home at the stroke of midnight; I didn't like drinking mash; I didn't have sex. I read books and had an inferiority complex because I was afraid to do all that other stuff. I don't know anything about being a badass punk rocker.

It's the same thing with the story about the engine room kids—what do I know about child labor? What do I know about how kids relate to each other under circumstances like that? Not to mention, what do I know about spaceships? I'm talking out of my ass.

So there I am. I can't write about what I know, and I can't write about what I don't know. Better yet, I've told everyone that I'm staying in Åre until I've finished THE NOVEL. I somehow thought that saying it would make it happen.

Hang in there for another couple of weeks. And do what? Try some more. Go on biking trips and eat whey cheese.

6/2

I'm taking a break. I've scrapped everything I was working on. I rented a car and drove west over the border into Norway, where I bought ice cream in a lonely little kiosk. When I was a kid, I thought the sign in Norwegian that said *åpen*, open, meant *apan*, the monkey. It was the most hilarious thing ever.

I had my ice cream and looked at the Sylarna Mountains and the cotton-grass swaying on the bog. There was a thick herbal smell of mountain summer. Little pools and puddles were everywhere, absolutely clear, miniature John Bauer landscapes. I considered going on to Levanger, but it felt too far. I went for a swim in Gev Lake on the way home. It was just like when I was little: warm and shallow enough that if you walk out into the middle, the water only reaches your waist. Tiny minnows nibbled at my feet.

6/3

I'm having coffee in the little cabin on Åreskutan's Summit. It's a clear day, and I can see the mountain range undulating in the west, worn blunt by the ice ages. Mom once said that when she was a kid, there was a leathery old man who every morning hiked all the way up the mountain with a satchel full of coffee thermoses and cinnamon rolls that he would sell in the cabin. This was before the cableway, somewhere in the 1950s. The old man had done that since time immemorial, even when my grandmother and her sister were kids and dragged baking troughs up the mountain to ride them down like sleds.

6/4

I went for a walk in the holiday village. I became a little obsessed with the thought of stuff you can do when nobody's looking. Build a pillow fort outside cottage number six. Streak howling through the street. I was thinking specifically of howling when I spotted the pupae. They're the size of my fist now. That was fast. I forgot to tell Brita. Of course, I had to touch one of them again. It felt warmer than my hand.

Went shopping in Kall, had a cup of coffee, bought the newspaper, went past Brita's house. I told her about the pupae. Her reaction was pretty strange. She said something about the pupae sitting there in summer, and that I should leave them alone. That's why she'd put me in the cottage outside the village, so that the pupae would be left in peace. Yes, yes, I said. I won't do anything. Do promise you won't do anything, said Brita, and suddenly she was pleading. They have nowhere else to go, she said; you're family, I can trust you can't I? Yes, yes, I said, I promise. I have no idea what she's on about.

6/5

I dreamed that there was a scraping noise by the door. Someone was looking in through the little side window. It was human-shaped, but it sort of had no detail. It was waving at me with a fingerless paw. The door handle was jerking up and down. The creature on the other side said nothing. It just smiled and waved. The door handle bobbed up and down, up and down.

It's five past ten. I've slept for almost ten hours.

I went into the village to check if the pupae had grown, but all that remains are some empty skins hanging under the eaves. So that's that.

6/6

There's a knock on the door and someone's waving at me through the side window. It's a middle-aged man. When I open the door, he presents himself as Sigvard and shakes my hand. He's one of the groups of tourists who live here during the summer. They've rented all the cabins, and now they're throwing a party, and they've seen me sitting alone in my cottage. Would I like to join them? There's plenty of food for everyone. I'm very welcome.

The party takes place in the little assembly hall. People are strolling over there from the other cabins. They're dressed up for a summer night's party: the women in party dresses and lusekofte sweaters tied over their shoulders, the men in slacks and bright windbreakers. Inside, the assembly hall is decked with yellow lanterns, and a long buffet table lines one of the walls. The guests are of all ages and resemble one another. I ask Sigvard if they're family, and Sigvard says yes, they are! It's a big family meet-up, the Nilssons, and they stay here a few weeks every summer. And now it's time to eat.

The buffet table is covered in dishes from every holiday of the year: steak, roast ham, tjälknul, hot cloudberries, new potatoes, patés, pickled herring, gravlax, lutefisk, seven kinds of cookies, cake. I'm starving. I go for second and third helpings. The food has no taste, but the texture is wonderful, especially the ice cream mingled with hot cloudberries. Everyone seems very interested in me. They want to know about my family. When I tell them that Brita is my great-aunt, they cheer and say that we're related, then; I belong to the Anders branch of the family. Dear Brita! They love her! I'll always be welcome here. Everyone else here belongs to the Anna branch: Anna, Anders's sister and the eldest daughter of the patriarch Mats Nilsson.

When we're done eating, it's time to dance. The raspy stereo plays dansband music: singers croon about smiling golden-brown eyes, accompanied by an innocent and sickly sweet tune. Everyone takes to the dance floor. Sigvard asks me to dance. This is like a cliché of Swedish culture, I say without thinking. Yes, isn't it, Sigvard says, and smiles. He holds me close. Then I wake up.

6/8

I started writing again. Throwing the old stuff out worked. Something else has surfaced—it's fairly incoherent, but it's a story, and I'm not about to ruin it by looking too closely at it. It has nothing to do with teenage trouble at Hunddagis, or *Lord of the Flies* with kids in spaceships. It's about my own family in Åre, a sort of pseudo-documentary. Some mixed memories of my grandmother's and mother's stories of life up here, woven together with my own fantasies to form a third story. Above all else, I'm having *fun*. I refuse to think about editing. I write and stare out over Kall Lake.

The dreams are a sign that things are happening—I keep dreaming about the same things, and it's very clear, very detailed. It's the same scenario as before, that is, Sigvard knocking on the door and taking me to the assembly hall. We eat enormous amounts of food and dance to dansband classics. I talk to all my relatives. They tell stories about Mats Nilsson's eldest daughter and how she started the new branch of the family when she married and moved north from Åre. I don't remember those stories when I wake up.

6/13

I started with Mother's stories, continued with Gran's generation, and am working my way back in time to form a sort of backward history. I wrote about the war and how Great-Gran smuggled shoes and lard to occupied Norway. Then I wrote about how Gran met Grandpa and moved down to Stockholm. Right now Gran is a teenager, it's the twenties, and she's making her first bra out of two stocking heels because she can't afford to buy a real one. She and her sister are getting ready to go to a dance in Järpen. It's an hour's bike ride. I'm looking forward to writing the story about my great-great-grandfather who built a church organ out of a kitchen sofa. Some things you can't make up.

The dreams change a little each night. I've discovered that I have a fair amount of control of my actions. I wander around in the cabins and talk to the inhabitants. In true dream fashion, they all come from little villages with names that don't exist like Höstvåla, Bräggne, Ovart; all located somewhere north of Åre, by the lakes that pool between the mountains.

Sigvard's wife is called Ingrid. They have three teenage children.

6/15

I'm a little disgusted by the direction this is all taking. I don't know how to interpret what's going on. The front doors are always unlocked; I go where I wish. Last night and the night before last, it happened several times that I walked into a house and people were having sex. On all surfaces, like kitchen tables or sofas. They greet me politely when I open the door and then go back to, not making love, but fucking. Nobody seems particularly into it. They might as well be chopping onions or cleaning the floors. In and out and the flat smack of flesh on flesh. And it's everyone on everyone: man and wife, father and daughter, mother and son, sister and brother. But always in heterosexual configurations. I asked Sigvard what they were doing. We're multiplying, he said. That's what people do.

6/20

It's midsummer. I've managed just over eighty pages. I've gotten as far back as great-great-great-grandfather Anders, son of Mats Nilsson, and if I want to get even further back, I'll have to do some research on Anders's five siblings or just ramble out into fairy-tale country. Not that making stuff up seems to be a problem. There's no end to it. I've gone back to the start to fill in holes, like Mother and Gran's siblings. No editing just yet, just more material. Brita asked me if I wanted to come with her to celebrate midsummer. I declined. All I want to do is write. Besides, it's freezing outside, and the gnats are out in full force. It'd be a good idea, research-wise, to see Brita, but I don't feel like being around people.

6/21

Sigvard came knocking on my door. He was wearing a wreath of flowers and held a schnapps glass in one hand. We danced to dansband music, the legendary Sven-Ingvars; we competed in sack racing and three-legged racing. Most of the women and girls had large, rounded bellies and moved awkwardly. When the dancing and playing was over, we ate new potatoes and pickled herring, little meatballs and sausages, fresh strawberries with cream, toasting one another with schnapps spiced with cumin and wormwood. It'll get darker now, said Sigvard. He burst into tears. Yes, I replied. But why is that so terrible? It makes me think of death, he said.

7/1

One hundred fifty pages! That's an average of five pages a day. Very well done. The last ten days have been about putting more meat on the bones I finished building around midsummer. In other words, embroidering what facts I had with more ideas of my own. Editing is going to take a lot longer, but I have a solid structure from beginning to end—no bothersome gaps or holes.

I decided to stop at Anders. I need to check the other siblings now, especially Anna. I've tried to talk to Brita, but she's always busy whenever I come over. I'm done with this place, though. I'm homesick. I've booked a ticket to Stockholm for the sixth. I can go back home with a good conscience.

7/4

They're weeping and wailing. They're all dressed in black. They won't say why. I've told them I'll be leaving soon, but I don't think that's why they're sad.

7/5

I finally caught Brita for a cup of coffee. She apologized for being so busy. I asked her about Mats Nilsson's children, but she doesn't know much outside our own branch. Still, I asked her if she knew anything about Anna, the eldest daughter. Not much, she said. But then there wasn't much to know about her. She disappeared without a trace when she was twenty years old. The consensus was that she probably drowned herself in Kall Lake or in one of the sinkholes in the quarry. In any case, she was never seen again.

7/6

I'm leaving on the night train. I cleaned out the cottage; all that's left is to hand over the keys to Brita.

Sigvard knocked on the door in my dream. The whole village was crowding behind him. They looked aged and crumpled somehow, and they were weeping loudly. Some of them didn't seem to be able to walk on their own—they were crawling around. Sigvard came in first; he dropped to his knees and flung his arms around my legs. I sat down on the floor. He put his head in my lap. My dear, he said. It was the best summer ever. We're so grateful. Then he sighed and lay still. The others came, one by one. They lay down around me and curled up. They sighed and lay still. I patted their heads. There, there, I said. Go to sleep now, go to sleep. Their bodies were like light shells. They collapsed in on themselves.

I was woken up just after seven by an ice-cold draft. The front door was open. I went for a last walk in the village. Clusters of tiny spheres hang under the eaves.

Reindeer Mountain

CILLA WAS TWELVE YEARS OLD the summer Sara put on her great-grandmother's wedding dress and disappeared up the mountain. It was in the middle of June, during summer break. The drive was a torturous nine hours, interrupted much too rarely by bathroom and ice-cream breaks. Cilla was reading in the passenger seat of the ancient Saab, Sara stretched out in the backseat, Mom driving. They were traveling northwest on gradually narrowing roads, following the river, the towns shrinking and the mountains drawing closer. Finally, the old Saab crested a hill and rolled down into a wide valley where the river pooled into a lake between two mountains. Cilla put her book down and looked out the window. The village sat between the lake and the great hump of Reindeer Mountain, its lower reaches covered in dark pine forest. The mountain on the other side of the lake was partly deforested, as if someone had gone over it with a giant electric shaver. Beyond them, more shapes undulated toward the horizon, shapes rubbed soft by the ice ages.

"Why does no one live on the mountain itself?" Sara suddenly said, pulling one of her earphones out. Robert Smith's voice leaked into the car.

"It's not very convenient, I suppose," said Mom. "The hillside is very steep."

"Nana said it's because the mountain belongs to the *vittra.*"

"She would." Mom smirked. "It sounds much more exciting. Look!"

She pointed up to the hillside on the right. A rambling two-story house sat in a meadow outside the village. "There it is."

Cilla squinted at the house. It sat squarely in the meadow. Despite the faded paint and angles that were slightly off, it somehow seemed very solid. "Are we going there now?"

"No. It's late. We'll go straight to Aunt Hedvig's and get ourselves settled. But you can come with me tomorrow if you like. The cousins will all be meeting to see what needs doing."

"I can't believe you're letting the government buy the land," said Sara.

"We're not letting them," sighed Mom. "They're expropriating."

"Forcing us to sell," Cilla said.

"I know what it means, smart-ass," Sara muttered, and kicked the back of the passenger seat. "It still blows."

Cilla reached back and pinched her leg. Sara caught her hand and twisted her fingers until Cilla squealed. They froze when the car suddenly braked. Mom killed the engine and glared at them.

"Get out," she said. "Hedvig's cottage is up this road. You can walk the rest of the way. I don't care who started," she continued when Cilla opened her mouth to protest. "Get out. Walk it off."

They arrived at Hedvig's cottage too tired to bicker. The house sat on a slope above the village, red with white window frames and a little porch overlooking the village and lake. Mom was in the kitchen with Hedvig. They were having coffee, slurping it through a lump of sugar between their front teeth.

"I've spoken to Johann about moving him into a home," said Hedvig as the girls came in. "He's not completely against it. But he wants to stay here. And there is no home here that can handle people with ... nerve problems. And he can't stay with Otto forever." She looked up at Cilla and Sara and smiled, her eyes almost disappearing in a network of wrinkles. She looked very much like Nana and Mom, with the same wide cheekbones and slanted gray eyes.

"Look at you lovely girls!" said Hedvig, getting up from the table.

She was slightly hunchbacked and very thin. Embracing her, Cilla could feel her vertebrae through the cardigan.

Hedvig urged them to sit down. "They're store-bought. I hope you don't mind," she said, setting a plate of cookies on the table.

Hedvig and Mom continued to talk about Johann. He was the eldest brother of Hedvig and Nana, the only one of the siblings to remain in the family house. He had lived alone in there for forty years. Mom and her cousins had the summer to get Johann out and salvage whatever they could before the demolition crew came. No one quite knew what the house looked like inside. Johann hadn't let anyone in for decades.

. . .

There were two guest rooms in the cottage. Sara and Cilla shared a room under the eaves; Mom took the other with the threat that any fighting would mean her moving in with her daughters. The room was small but cozy, with lacy white curtains and dainty furniture, like in an oversize doll's house: two narrow beds with white throws, a writing desk with curved legs, two slim-backed chairs. It smelled of dried flowers and dust. The house had no toilet. Hedvig showed a bewildered Cilla to an outhouse across the little meadow. Inside, the outhouse was clean and bare, with a little candle and matches, even a magazine holder. The rich scent of decomposing waste clung to the back of the nose. Cilla went quickly, imagining an enormous cavern under the seat, full of spiders and centipedes and evil clowns.

When she got back, she found Sara already in bed, listening to music with her eyes closed. Cilla got into her own bed. The sheets were rough, the pillowcase embroidered with someone's initials. She picked up her book from the nightstand. She was reading it for the second time, enjoying slowly and with relish the scene where the heroine tries on a whalebone corset. After a while she took her glasses off, switched off the lamp and lay on her back. It was almost midnight, but cold light filtered through the curtains. Cilla sat up again, put her glasses on and pulled a curtain aside. The town lay tiny and quiet on the shore of the lake, the mountain beyond backlit by the eerie glow of the sun skimming just below the horizon. The sight brought a painful sensation Cilla could neither name nor explain. It was like a longing, worse than anything she had ever experienced, but for *what* she had no idea. Something tremendous waited out there. Something wonderful was going to happen, and she was terrified that she would miss it.

Sara had fallen asleep, her breathing deep and steady. The Cure trickled out from her earphones. It was a song Cilla liked. She got back into bed and closed her eyes, listening to Robert sing of hands in the sky for miles and miles.

Cilla was having breakfast in the kitchen when she heard the crunch of boots on gravel through the open front door. Mom sat on the doorstep in faded jeans and clogs and her huge gray cardigan, a cup in her hands. She set it down and rose to greet the visitor. Cilla rose from the table and peeked outside. Johann wasn't standing very close to Mom, but it was as if he was towering over her. He wore a frayed blue anorak that hung loose on his thin frame, his grime-encrusted work trousers tucked into green rubber boots. His face lay in thick wrinkles like old leather, framed by a shock of white hair. He gave off a rancid, goatlike odor that made Cilla put her hand over her nose and mouth. If Mom was bothered by it, she didn't let on.

"About time you came back, *stå'års*," he said. He called her a girl. No one had called Mom a girl before. "It's been thirty years. Did you forget about us?"

"Of course not, Uncle," said Mom. "I just chose to live elsewhere, that's all." Her tone was carefully neutral.

Johann leaned closer to Mom. "And you came back just to help tear the house down. You're a hateful little bitch. No respect for the family."

If Mom was upset, she didn't show it. "You know that we don't have a choice. And it's not okay to talk to me like that, Johann."

Johann's eyes softened. He looked down at his boots. "I'm tired," he said.

"I know," said Mom. "Are you comfortable at Otto's?"

Cilla must have made a noise, because Johann turned his head toward her. He stuck out his hand in a slow wave. "Oh, hello there. Did you bring both children, Marta? How are they? Any of them a little strange? Good with music? Strange dreams? Monsters under the bed?" He grinned. His teeth were a brownish yellow.

"You need to go now, Johann," said Mom.

"Doesn't matter if you move south," Johann said. "Can't get it out of your blood." He left, rubber boots crunching on the gravel path.

Mom wrapped her cardigan more tightly around herself and came inside.

"What was that about?" Cilla said.

"Johann has all sorts of ideas."

"Is he talking about why we have so much craziness in the family?"

"Johann thinks it's a curse." She smiled at Cilla and patted her cheek. "He's very ill. We're sensitive, that's all. We have to take care of ourselves."

Cilla leaned her forehead against Mom's shoulder. Her cardigan smelled of wool and cold air. "What if me or Sara gets sick?"

"Then we'll handle it," said Mom. "You'll be fine."

What everyone knew was this: that sometime in the late nineteenth century a woman named Märet came down from the mountain and married Jacob Jonsson. They settled in

Jacob's family home, and she bore him several children, most of whom survived to adulthood, although not unscathed. According to the story, Märet was touched. She saw strange things and occasionally did and said strange things, too. Märet's children, and their children in turn, were plagued by frail nerves and hysteria; people applied more modern terms as time passed.

Alone of all her siblings, Cilla's mother had no symptoms. That was no guarantee, of course. Ever since Cilla had been old enough to understand what the story really meant, she had been waiting for her or Sara to catch it, *that*, the disease. Mom said they weren't really at risk, since Dad's family had no history of mental illness, and anyway they had grown up in a stable environment. Nurture would triumph over nature. Negative thinking was not allowed. It seemed, though, as if Sara might continue the tradition.

Sara was sitting under the bed covers with her back to the wall, eyes closed, Robert Smith wailing in her earphones. She opened her eyes when Cilla shut the door.

"Johann was here." Cilla wrinkled her nose. "He smells like goat."

"Okay," said Sara. Her eyes were a little glazed.

"Are you all right?"

Sara rubbed her eyes. "It's the thing."

Cilla sat next to her on the bed, taking Sara's hand. She was cold, her breathing shallow; Cilla could feel the pulse hammering in her wrist. Sara was always a little on edge, but sometimes it got worse. She had said that it felt like something horrible was about to happen, but she couldn't say exactly what, just a terrible sense of doom. It had started about six months ago, about the same time that she got her first period.

"Want me to get Mom?" Cilla said as always.

"No. It's not that bad," said Sara, as usual. She leaned back against the wall, closing her eyes.

Sara had lost it once in front of Mom. Mom didn't take it well. She had told Sara to snap out of it, that there was nothing wrong with her, that she was just having hysterics. After that, Sara kept it to herself. In this, if in nothing else, Cilla was allowed to be her confidante. In a way, Mom was right: compared to paranoid schizophrenia, a little anxiety wasn't particularly crazy. Not that it helped Sara any.

"You can pinch me if it makes you feel better." Cilla held out her free arm. She always did what she could to distract Sara.

"Brat."

"Ass."

Sara smiled a little. She looked down at Cilla's hand in hers, suddenly wrenching it around so that it landed on her sister's leg.

"Why are you hitting yourself? Stop hitting yourself!" she shouted in mock horror.

There was a knock on the door. Mom opened it without waiting for an answer. She was dressed in rubber boots and a bright yellow raincoat over her cardigan. "I'm going to the house now, if you want to come."

"Come on, brat," said Sara, letting go of Cilla's hand.

The driveway up to the house was barely visible under the weeds. Two middle-aged men in windbreakers and rubber boots were waiting in the front yard. Mom pointed at them.

"That's Otto and Martin!" Mom waved at them through the window.

"I thought there were six cousins living up here," said Sara.

"There are," said Mom. "But the others aren't well. It's just Otto and Martin today."

They stepped out into cold, wet air. Cilla was suddenly glad of her thick jeans and knitted sweater. Sara, who had refused to wear any of the (stupid and embarrassing) sweaters Mom offered, was shivering in her black tights and thin long-sleeved shirt.

The cousins greeted each other with awkward hugs. Otto and Martin were in their fifties, both with the drawn-out Jonsson look: tall and sinewy with watery blue eyes, a long jaw, and wide cheekbones. Martin was a little shorter and younger, with fine black hair that stood out from his head like a dark dandelion. Otto, balding and with a faraway look, only nodded and wouldn't shake hands.

This close, the old house looked ready to fall apart. The red paint was flaking in thick layers, the steps up to the front door warped. Some of the windowpanes were covered with bits of white plastic and duct tape.

Mom waved toward the house. "Johann's not with you?"

Martin shrugged, taking a set of keys from his pocket. "He didn't want to be here for this. All right. We'll start with going through the rooms one by one, seeing what we can salvage. Otto has pen and paper to make a list."

"You haven't been in here until now?" said Mom.

"We've been cleaning a little. Johann only used a couple of the rooms, but it was bad. The smell should be bearable now."

Otto opened the door. Johann's unwashed stench wafted

out in a sour wave. "You get used to it." He ducked his head under the lintel and went inside.

Johann had used two rooms and the kitchen on the ground floor. Neither Cilla nor Sara could bring themselves to enter them, the stench of filth and rot so strong it made them gag. By the light coming in through the door, Cilla could see piles of what looked like rags, stacks of newspapers, and random furniture.

"There was a layer of milk cartons and cereal boxes this high on the floors in there," said Martin, pointing to his knee. "The ones at the bottom were from the seventies."

"I don't think he ate much else," Otto filled in. "He refuses to eat anything but cornflakes and milk at my house. He says all other food is poisoned."

Otto, Martin, and Mom looked at one another.

Mom shrugged. "That's how it is."

Otto sucked air in between pursed lips, the quiet *jo* that acknowledged and ended the subject.

The smell wasn't as bad in the rest of the house; Johann seemed to have barricaded himself in his two rooms. The sitting room was untouched. Daylight filtered in through filthy windowpanes, illuminating furniture that looked handmade and ancient: cabinets painted with flower designs, a wooden sofa with a worn seat, a rocking chair with the initials OJ and the date 1898.

"It looks just like when we were kids," said Mom.

"Doesn't it?" said Otto.

Cilla returned to the entryway, peering up the stairs to the next floor. "What about upstairs? Can we go upstairs?"

"Certainly," said Martin. "Let me go first and turn on the lights." He took a torch from his pocket, lighting his way as he walked up the stairs. Sara and Cilla followed him.

The top of the stairs ended in a narrow corridor, where doors opened to the master bedroom and two smaller rooms with two beds in each.

"How many people lived here?" Cilla peered into the master bedroom.

"Depends on when you mean," Martin replied. "Your grandmother had four siblings altogether. And I think there was at least a cousin or two of theirs living here during harvest, too."

"But there are only four single beds," said Sara from the doorway of another room.

Martin shrugged. "People shared beds."

"But you didn't live here all the time, right?"

"No, no. My mother moved out when she got married. I grew up in town. Everyone except Johann moved out."

"There are more stairs over here," said Sara from farther away.

"That's the attic," said Martin. "You can start making lists of things up there." He handed Cilla his torch, a pen, and a sheaf of paper. "Mind your step."

The attic ran the length of the house, divided into compartments. Each compartment was stacked with stuff: boxes, furniture, old skis, kick-sleds, a bicycle. The little windows and the weak lightbulb provided enough light that they didn't need the torch. Cilla started in one end of the attic, Sara in the other, less sorting and more rooting around. After a while, Mom came upstairs.

"There's a huge chest here," said Sara after a while, pushing a stack of boxes to the side.

Cilla left her list and came over to look. It was a massive blue chest with a rounded lid, faded and painted with flowers.

"Let me see," said Mom from behind them.

Mom came forward, knelt in front of the chest, and opened it, the lid lifting with a groan. It was filled almost to the brim with neatly folded white linen, sprinkled with mothballs. In a corner sat some bundles wrapped in tissue paper.

Mom shone her torch into the chest. "This looks like a hope chest." She carefully lifted the tissue paper and uncovered red wool. She handed the torch to Cilla, using both hands to lift the fabric up. It was a full-length skirt, the cloth untouched by vermin.

"Pretty," said Sara. She took the skirt, holding it up to her waist.

"There's more in here," said Mom, moving tissue paper aside. "A shirt, an apron, and a shawl. A whole set. It could be Märet's."

"Like what she got married in?" said Cilla.

"Maybe so," said Mom.

"It's my size," said Sara. "Can I try it on?"

"Not now. Keep doing lists." Mom took the skirt back, carefully folding it and putting it back into the chest.

Sara kept casting glances at the chest the rest of the morning. When Cilla caught her looking, Sara gave her the finger.

Later in the afternoon, Mom emptied a cardboard box and put the contents from the hope chest in it. "I'm taking this over to Hedvig's. I'm sure she can tell us who it belonged to."

After dinner, Mom unpacked the contents of the hope chest in Hedvig's kitchen. There were six bundles in all: the red skirt with a matching bodice, a red shawl, a white linen shift, a long apron striped in red and black, and a black purse embroidered with red flowers. Hedvig picked up the purse and ran a finger along the petals.

"This belonged to Märet." Hedvig smiled. "She showed me these once, before she passed away. That's what she wore when she came down from the mountain," she said. "I thought they were gone. I'm very glad you found them."

"How old were you when she died?" said Sara.

"It was in twenty-one, so I was fourteen. It was terrible." Hedvig shook her head. "She died giving birth to Nils, your youngest great-uncle. It was still common back then."

Cilla fingered the skirt. Out in daylight, the red wool was bright and luxurious, like arterial blood. "What was she like?"

Hedvig patted the purse. "Märet was . . . a peculiar woman," she said eventually.

"Was she really crazy?" Cilla said.

"Crazy? I suppose she was. She certainly passed something on. The curse, like Johann says. But that's silly. She came here to help with harvest, you know, and she fell in love with your great-grandfather. He didn't know much about her. No one did, except that she was from somewhere northeast of here."

"I thought she came down from the mountain," I said.

Hedvig smiled. "Yes, she would say that when she was in the mood."

"What about those things, anyway?" Sara said. "Are they fairies?"

"What?" Hedvig gave her a blank look.

"The *vittra*," Cilla filled in helpfully. "The ones that live on the mountain."

"Eh," said Hedvig. "Fairies are cute little things that prance about in meadows. The *vittra* look like humans, but taller and more handsome. And it's *inside* the mountain, not on it." She had brightened visibly, becoming more animated as she spoke. "There were always stories about *vittra* living up there. Sometimes they came down to trade with the townspeople. You had to be careful with them, though. They could curse you or kill you if you crossed them. But they had the fattest cows, and the finest wool, and beautiful silver jewelry. Oh, and they liked to dress in red." Hedvig indicated the skirt Cilla had in her lap. "And sometimes they came to dance with the local young men and women, even taking one away for marriage. And when a child turned out to have nerve problems, they said it was because someone in the family had passed on *vittra* blood . . ."

"But did you meet any?" Sara blurted.

Hedvig laughed. "Of course not. There would be some odd folk showing up to sell their things in town, but they were mostly Norwegians or from those *really* small villages up north where everyone's their own uncle."

Sara burst out giggling.

"Auntie!" Mom looked scandalized.

Hedvig waved a hand at her. "I'm eighty-seven years old. I can say whatever I like."

"But what about Märet?" Cilla leaned forward.

"Mother, yes." Hedvig poured a new cup of coffee, arm trembling under the weight of the thermos. "She was a bit strange, I suppose. She really *was* tall for a woman, and she would say strange things at the wrong time, talk to animals, things like that. People would joke about *vittra* blood."

"What do you think?" said Sara.

"I think she must have had a hard life, to run away from her family and never speak of them again." Hedvig gently took the skirt from Cilla and folded it.

"But the red . . ."

Hedvig shook her head and smiled. "It was an expensive color back then. Saying someone wore red meant they were rich. This probably cost Märet a lot." She put the clothes back in the cardboard box and closed it.

Cilla stayed up until she was sure everyone else had gone to bed. It took ages. Sara wrote in her journal until one o' clock and then took some time to fall asleep, Robert Smith still whining in her ears.

The cardboard box was sitting on the kitchen sofa, the silk paper in a pile next to it. Cilla lifted the lid, uncovering red wool that glowed in the half dawn. The shift and the skirt were too long and very tight around the stomach. She kept the skirt unbuttoned and rolled the waistline down, hoisting it so the hem wouldn't trip her up. She tied the apron tight around her waist to hold everything up and clipped the purse onto the apron string. The bodice was too loose on her flat chest and wouldn't close at the waist, so she let it hang open and tied the shawl over her shoulders.

It was quiet outside, the horizon glowing an unearthly gold, the rest of the sky shifting in blue and green. The birds were quiet. The moon was up, a tiny crescent in the middle of the sky. The air was cold and wet; the grass swished against the skirt, leaving moisture pearling on the wool. Cilla could see all the way down to the lake and up to the mountain. She took her glasses off and put them in the purse. Now she was one of the *vittra*, coming down from the mountain, heading for the river. She was tall and graceful, her step quiet. She danced as she went, barefoot in the grass.

A sliver of sun peeking over the horizon broke the spell. Cilla's feet were suddenly numb with cold. She went back into the house and took everything off again, fished her glasses out, and folded the clothes into the cardboard box. It was good wool; the dew brushed off without soaking into the skirt. When Cilla slipped into bed again, it was only a little past two. The linen was warm and smooth against the cold soles of her feet.

They returned to the family house the following day. Sara decided that wading through debris in the attic was stupid and sulked on a chair outside. Cilla spent the day writing more lists. She found more skis, some snowshoes, a cream separator, dolls, a half-finished sofa bed, and a sewing table that was in almost perfect condition.

Johann showed up in the afternoon. Martin and Otto seemed to think he was going to make a scene, because they walked out and met him far down the driveway. Eventually they returned, looking almost surprised, with Johann walking beside them, his hands clasped behind his back. When Cilla next saw him, he had sat down in a chair next to Sara. Sara had a shirtsleeve over her nose and mouth, but she was listening to him talk with rapt attention. Johann left again soon after. Sara wouldn't tell Cilla what they'd spoken about, but her eyes were a little wider than usual, and she kept knocking things over.

When they returned to Hedvig's house, Sara decided to try on Märet's dress. On her, the skirt wasn't too long or too tight; it cinched her waist just so, ending neatly at her ankle. The bodice fit like it was tailor-made for her as well, tracing the elegant tapering curve of her back from shoulder to hip.

She looked like she'd just stepped out of a story. It made Cilla's chest feel hollow.

Sara caught her gaze in the mirror and made a face. "It looks stupid." She plucked at the skirt. "The red is way too bright. I wonder if you could dye it black? Because that would look awesome."

Cilla looked at her own reflection, just visible beyond Sara's red splendor. She was short and barrel-shaped, eyes tiny behind her glasses. There were food stains on her sweater. "*You* look stupid," she managed.

Mom was scrubbing potatoes in the kitchen when Cilla came downstairs.

"Who's getting the dress, Mom? Because Sara wants to dye it black."

"Oh ho?" said Mom. "Probably not, because it's not hers."

"Can I have it?" Cilla shifted her weight from foot to foot. "I wouldn't do anything to it."

"No, love. It belongs to Hedvig."

"But she's *old*. She won't use it."

Mom turned and gave Cilla a long look, eyebrows low. "It belonged to her *mother*, Cilla. How would you feel if you found my wedding dress and someone gave it away to some relative instead?"

"She has everything else," Cilla said. "I don't have anything from Great-Gran."

"I'm sure we can find something from the house," said Mom. "But not the dress. It means a lot to Hedvig. Think of someone else's feelings for a change."

Sara came down a little later with the same request. Mom yelled at her.

. . .

Maybe it was because of Mom's outburst, but Sara became twitchier as the evening passed on. Finally she muttered something about going for a walk and shrugged into her jacket. Cilla hesitated a moment and then followed.

"Fuck off," Sara muttered without turning her head when Cilla came running after her.

"No way," said Cilla.

Sara sighed and rolled her eyes. She increased her pace until Cilla had to half jog to keep up. They said nothing until they came down to the lake's shore, a stretch of rounded river stones that made satisfying billiard-ball noises under Cilla's feet.

Sara sat down on one of the larger rocks and dug out a soft ten-pack of cigarettes. She shook one out and lit it. "Tell Mom and I'll kill you."

"I know." Cilla sat down next to her. "Why are you being so weird? Ever since you talked to Johann."

Sara took a drag on her cigarette and blew the smoke out through her nose. She shrugged. Her eyes looked wet. "He made me understand some things, is all."

"Like what?"

"Like I'm not crazy. Like none of us are." She looked out over the lake. "We should stay here. Maybe we'd survive." Her eyes really were wet now. She wiped at them with her free hand.

Cilla felt cold trickle down her back. "What are you on about?"

Sara rubbed her forehead. "You have to promise not to tell anyone, because if you tell anyone, bad stuff will happen, okay? Shit is going to happen just because I'm telling *you*. But I'll tell you because you're my little sis." She slapped a quick rhythm on her thigh. "Okay. So it's like this—the world is going to end soon. It's going to end in ninety-six."

Cilla blinked. "How would you know?"

"It's in the newspapers, if you look. The Gulf War, yeah? That's when it started. Saddam Hussein is going to take revenge and send nukes, and then the U.S. will nuke back, and then Russia jumps in. And then there'll be nukes everywhere, and we're dead. Or we'll die in the nuclear winter, 'cause they might not nuke Sweden, but there'll be nothing left for us." Sara's eyes were a little too wide.

"Okay," Cilla said slowly. "But how do you *know* all this is going to happen?"

"I can see the signs. In the papers. And I just . . . know. Like someone told me. The twenty-third of February in ninety-six, that's when the world ends. I mean, haven't you noticed that something's really, really *wrong*?"

Cilla dug her toe into the stones. "It's the opposite."

"What." There was no question mark to Sara's tone.

"Something wonderful," Cilla said. Her cheeks were hot. She focused her eyes on her toe.

"You're a fucking idiot." Sara turned her back, demonstratively, and lit a new cigarette.

Cilla never could wait her out. She walked back home alone.

On midsummer's eve, they had a small feast. There was pickled herring and new potatoes, smoked salmon, fresh strawberries and cream, spiced schnapps for Mom and Hedvig. It was past ten when Cilla pulled on Sara's sleeve.

"We have to go pick seven kinds of flowers," she said.

Sara rolled her eyes. "That's kid stuff. I have a headache," she said, standing up. "I'm going to bed."

Cilla remained at the table with her mother and great-aunt, biting her lip.

Mom slipped an arm around her shoulder. "Picking seven flowers is an old, old tradition," she said. "There's nothing silly about it."

"I don't feel like it anymore," Cilla mumbled.

Mom chuckled gently. "Well, if you change your mind, tonight is when you can stay up for as long as you like."

"Just be careful," said Hedvig. "The *vittra* might be out and about." She winked conspiratorially at Cilla.

At Hedvig's dry joke, Cilla suddenly knew with absolute certainty what she had been pining for, that wonderful *something* waiting out there. She remained at the table, barely able to contain her impatience until Mom and Hedvig jointly decided to go to bed.

Mom kissed Cilla's forehead. "Have a nice little midsummer's eve, love. I'll leave the cookies out."

Cilla made herself smile at her mother's patronizing remark and waited for the house to go to sleep.

She had put the dress on right this time, as well as she could, and clutched seven kinds of flowers in her left hand—buttercup, clover, geranium, catchfly, bluebells, chickweed, and daisies. She stood at the back of the house, on the slope facing the mountain. It was just past midnight, the sky a rich blue tinged with green and gold. The air had a sharp and herbal scent. It was very quiet.

Cilla raised her arms. "I'm ready," she whispered. In the silence that followed, she thought she could hear snatches of music. She closed her eyes and waited. When she opened them again, the *vittra* had arrived.

They came out from between the pine trees, walking in pairs, all dressed in red and white: the women wore red skirts and shawls and the men long red coats. Two of them were playing the fiddle, a slow and eerie melody in a minor key.

A tall man walked at the head of the train, dressed entirely in white. His hair was long and dark and very fine. There was something familiar about the shape of his face and the translucent blue of his eyes. For a moment, those eyes stared straight into Cilla's. It was like receiving an electric shock; it reverberated down into her stomach. Then he shifted his gaze and looked beyond her to where Sara was standing wide-eyed by the corner of the house in her over-size sleeping T-shirt. He walked past Cilla without sparing her another glance.

The beautiful man from the mountain approached Sara where she stood clutching the edge of the rain barrel. He put a hand on her arm and said something to her that Cilla couldn't hear. Whatever it was, it made Sara's face flood with relief. She took his hand, and they walked past Cilla to the rest of the group. The fiddle players started up their slow wedding march, and the procession returned to the mountain. Sara never looked back.

Cilla told them that Sara must have taken the dress, that she herself had gone to bed not long after the others. She told them of Sara's doomsday vision and her belief that she could tell the future by decoding secret messages in the newspaper. When the search was finally abandoned, the general opinion was that Sara had had a bout of psychotic depression and gone into the wild, where she had either fallen into a body of water or died of exposure somewhere she couldn't be found. Up there, you can die of hypothermia even in summer. Cilla said nothing of the procession, or of the plastic bag in her suitcase where Märet's dress lay cut into tiny strips.

She kept the bag for a long time.

Cloudberry Jam

I MADE YOU IN A TIN CAN. It was one of the unlabeled mystery cans the charity in Åre village handed out. Most of the time it would be sausages or split pea soup.

This is how I did it: I waited until it was my time of the month. I took the tin can from the shelf under the sink. I filled it halfway with fresh water and put half a teaspoon of salt in it. Next I put in a small, gnarled carrot from last year's garden. I had saved it because it had two prongs, like little legs, and armlike stumps. Then I held the can between my legs and let some blood trickle into it. Finally, some of my spit. I put some plastic wrap over the opening. The rest of the night, I sat with the can in my lap and sang to you. That's how you were made, in October, as the first snow fell.

You grew steadily through the winter months. I sang to you and fed you small drops of milk. By Yule you were big enough that I moved you to a larger container, an old bucket. You started kicking then, I suppose because you finally had room to move around. You didn't need any nourishment other than milk, which was good because the charity in Åre had closed. I wouldn't go and ask for welfare money. I lived on last year's potatoes and roots, a bird here and there, cotton grass from the bog, and whatever I managed to steal from the shops.

The snow was slow melting that year. It wasn't until late May that the last of the snowdrifts at the back of the house finally disappeared. The little mountain birches were unfolding their first leaves. I lifted the cloth and saw that you were ready to come out. You were curled up in the bucket, perfectly formed, the liquid around you cloudy and brown. I lifted you out and dried you off with a towel.

It was perhaps half past three in the morning. On the porch, the air was sharp and clear. I could see all the way to the Norwegian border, to the Sylarna Mountains. Sunlight trickled over the worn mountaintops. I held you up.

"Welcome home," I said.

You opened your tiny eyes and looked out over the bog. We stood like that for a while.

Once out of the bucket, you grew quickly. The cloudberries ripened in August, covering the bog in flecks of gold. We picked them together. By then you were walking, your skin becoming thicker and darker in the sun. Although you couldn't carry anything with your stumpy arms, you were good at snagging the berries with your mouth and dropping them in the basket. I made cloudberry compote and jam. You could never have enough of the cloudberries. I remember you sitting at the kitchen table, golden jam everywhere, smacking loudly.

. . .

As autumn slid into winter, you learned to talk. Your voice was low and a little raspy, and you couldn't roll your Rs. We read together: old magazines, children's books I had saved. We played in the snow. I had a kneading trough that we rode down into the valley and I dragged back up. You burrowed into the drifts, shoveling the snow aside with your arm stumps and wriggling tunnels through the snow. On the eve of your first Yule, you wondered about your origins.

"Where did I come from?" you asked. "Where's my father?"

"You don't have one," I said. "I made you myself."

"Everyone has a father."

"Not everyone."

"Why did you make me?" you said.

"I made you so that I could love you," I said.

The snow melted, and we celebrated your first birthday. The frost left the ground. The days lengthened. You reached me to my waist and didn't want to sit in my lap or let me hug you. We had our first argument when you started digging in the kitchen garden just outside the house. I found you in the bottom of a crater of upturned earth and seedlings, rubbing the soil into your skin. I yelled at you for ruining my plants, and why would you do this.

"But it's because the soil is good here," you said.

"Dig wherever you want," I said. "But stay the hell away from the garden, or we won't have anything to eat."

"The soil isn't as good anywhere else. You don't get it."

Without another word, you waddled off to the birch copse

and dug under the trees the rest of the morning while I tried to salvage the kitchen garden. It was as if you dug away your anger, because after a while you came back with your little arms outstretched. We went inside and made lunch together and got soil and mud all over the floors.

You kept digging every day. Over by the bog, down on the slope toward the valley. It looked like we had voles or rabbits. You'd come home with things you'd unearthed: a broken saucer, part of a ski pole, little bits of bone, fool's gold.

When the weather became warm enough, I took you to Kall Lake to go night swimming. I used to go swimming in Kall Lake as a child. That was the best thing about summer.

You squealed in delight when you saw the rocky shore and the gray lake mirror. Once in the water you became frightened. It was too big and loose you said, too loose. You sat on the shore while I swam. You didn't like the rocks, either—they were too hard. You wanted to go home and dig. We didn't go back to Kall Lake.

The new batch of jam takes up a whole shelf. I think it'll stay there. I can't eat jam anymore. I'll still keep it here, though, just in case.

I suppose it was bound to happen. I woke up from an afternoon nap to find the cottage empty. I looked behind and inside the shed, in the copse of mountain birch huddling next to the house. You were nowhere to be found. Finally, I started calling for you. There was no answer. I thought perhaps you had fallen into a hole on the bog. New ones open every spring. I put my rubber boots on and went to look. I walked from the cottage and west toward Sylarna. I walked until the cottage disappeared from view, and then I turned north. I walked back and forth, calling you, until the sun dipped below the horizon. Then I turned back to the house.

You must have been digging all day. I found the hole by accident, kicking the kneading trough in frustration where it lay on the ground by the front steps. As it moved, I saw the hole. I called your name.

"Please come out," I said.

"I don't want to," you said, muffled.

"What are you doing down there?"

"Digging."

"Won't you please come out? I'll make us supper."

"I don't want to."

I went and got the shovel, setting it to the edge of the hole. But as soon as the shovel broke the ground, you screamed. I looked down. The soil was riddled with white root tendrils.

"You're hurting me!" you wailed.

I understood then.

"I'm so sorry, love," I said. "I am so sorry. I won't hurt you anymore, I promise."

I went back into the house and sat down at the kitchen table. I cried a little. Then I got the watering can from the garden and filled it with fresh water. I poured it over the ground by the hole. I could hear a giggle down there. That was the first time I'd heard you make that sound.

August is here. The cloudberries are still red; in a little while they will ripen to gold. I will pick as many as I can, for jam and compote. You haven't spoken since that day you burrowed into the ground. But there's a clutch of green leaves growing by the hole. When I water them, I can still hear faint laughter.

Pyret

[py:ret]
Description, Behavior, and History

WHEN NOT APPLIED to small and defenseless creatures, the word "pyre" describes a mysterious life form: *Pyret*, Swedish for "the little tyke." The word has all the characteristics of a euphemism, but nothing resembling an older name has turned up—possibly because it was taboo and in time forgotten, as is often the case. A name that evokes an image of something benevolent and harmless indicates both a form of worship and an underlying fear of its powers: an expression of love and an appeal for benevolence.* During

---

* Like gods and spirits, predators were often called by euphemisms to avoid bad luck or visits from said creatures. In some cases the euphemisms have replaced the taboo name in common usage. The Swedish word for wolf, *varg* (killer, strangler), was originally a euphemism for the taboo *ulv*; similarly, the euphemism for magpie, *skata* (the elon-

the years I have spent researching Pyret, it seems more and more likely that this mix of adoration and fear stems from its extremely alien nature.

A mimic and an infiltrator, Pyret mingles with and assumes the form of pack or herd animals, changing color and shape to match the others. From a distance it will look like an ordinary animal. It does not grow actual fur, eyes, or other extremities— the features are completely superficial, making it likely that its skin is covered by chromatophores, much like octopi and chameleons.

Although its feeding habits remain unknown, one thing is certain: Pyret does not behave like a predator. There are no records of it causing physical harm, although it insists on physical *contact*, which has traumatized a number of witnesses. Accounts of Pyret invariably describe a creature that tries to get close, cuddle, and sometimes even mate with the animal or person in question. The adult size of Pyret seems to be anything between a human and a cow. As for life span, no Pyre has been observed to die of old age; it has either wandered off or been slain by humans.

Pyret seems to have sought out and coexisted with the farmers of the Nordic countries for centuries. Swedish, Norwegian, and Finnish folklore is rife with stories about farmers discovering a fledgling Pyre in a litter of domesticated animals (Tilli, Pia: *Nordic Cryptids*, Basilisk Förlag, Helsinki 1989, p. 68), indicating that the parent places its

---

gated one), has replaced the original *skjora*. The word for bear shared by all Germanic languages (in Swedish *björn*) simply means "brown," a euphemism so old that it has acquired euphemisms of its own and the original name has been lost (although linguists through comparative studies have constructed a hypothetical root word in Proto-Indo-European).

spawn with other litters, cuckoo-style. However, Pyret is just as likely to appear in its adult form: there are numerous mentions of strange cows, goats, or sheep appearing in a flock overnight, rubbing up against the other animals. Their presence is often described as having a calming effect. Cows and goats will start producing prodigious amounts of milk, sheep will grow silky soft wool, and pigs fatten up even if food is scarce.

A Gift from the Gods

The earliest mention of Pyret occurs in the Icelandic saga *Alfdís saga*, in which Alfdís Sigurdardóttir divorces her husband Gunnlaug because he accidentally sets fire to their barn while drunk, "killing six cows and also *Freyr's pyril*,[*] thereby ruining their family" (Jónsson, Guðni: *Íslendinga sögur*, Reykjavík, 1946, book 25, p. 15). Alfdís complains bitterly about the loss of the *pyril* that she had reared from infancy, and which had kept her cattle happy and fat (Jónsson, p. 16). Because of the death of the *pyril*, Alfdís is exempt from the normal divorce penalty and retains the family's remaining possessions, while Gunnlaug is cast out of the community and left destitute (Jónsson, p. 18). Gunnlaug's punishment and the attribution of the *pyril* to Freyr, a god of fertility, indicate that it was considered a sacred creature.

This is the first and last mention in Icelandic literature. Afterward and up to modern times, stories and accounts of Pyret are confined to the northern and middle Scandinavian Peninsula, as far south as the *pyril* of Stavanger (Tilli, p. 69)

---

[*] Old Norse form of the word "pyre," still in use in Norwegian.

and as far east as Carelia under the name of *pienokainen**
(Tilli, p. 72). The majority of accounts, however, come from
the sparsely populated countryside of northern Sweden.

"The Devil's Cattle"

The Christianization of Scandinavia dethroned the Norse
gods but did little to wipe out belief in supernatural creatures, due in part to all the attention they were given by
the Church. The *pyril* of Norse faith moved into folklore,
where it became the cattle of the *vittra*, powerful beings that
live underground and in hills, similar to the *daoine sidhe* of
Ireland. The Church, seeing it as a very real threat, called
Pyret "the Devil's cattle" and warned the populace not to
have dealings with it. Doing so was considered witchcraft.
This had the opposite effect, as folklorist Ebbe Schön conjec-
tures: "If the Church made so much noise about them, these
creatures must indeed be powerful and therefore worthy of
worship" (Schön, Ebbe: *Älvor, vättar och andra väsen,* Rabén
Prisma, Stockholm, 1996, p. 16).

Between the fifteenth and seventeenth centuries, roughly
four hundred people were tried and executed for witchcraft
and witchcraft-related crimes.† Twelve instances mention
involvement with Pyret (Leijd, Carl: *Rättsprocessens avarter,*
Gothenburg: Meli Förlag, 1964, p. 223). Extensive notes from
a court case in 1702 concern one Anders of Kräkånger, who
was sentenced to death for harboring Pyret. To my knowl-

---

* Finnish: "tyke."

† The most common witchcraft-related crime was "illegal mingling":
young men consorting with female trolls and *vittra.*

edge, it is also the only trial where Pyret was present. Usually, Pyret would be killed on sight, but Anders of Kräkånger had reared his to such a monstrous size that no one dared touch it. Shaped like a bull, it strode into the courtroom together with Anders and refused to leave his side. The trial was very short, as during the proceedings, "the unholy creature constantly rubbed up against its owner, emitting warbling noises and upsetting those attending, causing many to weep with fear" (Leijd, p. 257). The court decreed that Anders's death sentence be carried out immediately but was not quite sure how to deal with Pyret. Anders himself solved this conundrum, offering to go willingly if the court in turn promised to set Pyret free after his death. Considering what he might otherwise command his beast to do, the court accepted this. Whether it intended to keep this promise, we will never know.

Anders of Kräkånger was taken to the block; his beast followed him like a dog and we dared not touch it, not even the priest. The moment the prisoner's head was severed from his neck, the creature let out a terrible howl, and all who heard it cowered in horror. The creature then fell over and did not move again. When evening fell, it had started to shrink, as when one pours salt on a snail. The remains were shoveled into a trough and burned along with the prisoner's body (Leijd, p. 258).

As Pyret constantly seeks out the company of other mammals, I suspect that sometimes it forms an attachment so strong that, like Anders of Kräkånger's bull, it cannot survive separation. Companionship—belonging to or with someone—seems an intrinsic part of its being.

The case of Anders of Kräkånger was to be the last in

the history of Pyret-related trials. The arrival of rationalism changed the face of Scandinavian faith and superstition in a way Christianity had not. Scientist Carl Linnaeus held a lecture in 1762 during which he reached the conclusion that belief in "Pyret, nixies, vittra and their ilk" is a warning sign of what happens to a people that do not concern themselves with science:

These creatures would lurk among cows and goats, haunt every nook, live with us like house cats; and superstition, witchcraft, and warding swarm around us like gnats (Levertin, Oscar: *Carl von Linné. Lectures,* Albert Bonniers Boktryckeri, Stockholm, 1910, p. 50).

Pyret was officially wiped out of existence. This did not stop it from appearing.

Sjungpastorn: The Singing Pastor of Hålträsket

Accounts of Pyret assuming human shape are nearly nonexistent. There are three possible reasons:

It is non-sentient. Observations of dead specimens may support this, as they universally mention gelatinous bodies with nothing resembling a brain, nervous system, or inner organs (see, for example, Widerberg, Emilia: *Folk Tales of the Macabre,* Bragi Press, Oxford 1954);

It prefers non-sentient mammals (see all aforementioned cases);

It is sentient and does frequently take human shape, but witnesses identify it as something else entirely, for example, a vittra, changeling, or troll.

One remarkable exception is documented in an eerie account from the nineteenth century about the entity known as Sjungpastorn.

Margareta Persson (1835–1892) was the schoolmistress of Hålträsket, a village located in the mid-north of Sweden. She kept a diary for most of her life, meticulously cataloging events and people of the village. After her death the diaries were donated to Umeå Heritage Museum.

In late November of 1867, during the last great famine in Scandinavia, Persson documented the passing of the local priest. No replacement came, and there was no easy way to travel elsewhere for Mass.

The cold deepened and the days shortened as the year drew toward its end. Two villagers killed themselves, one by hanging and one by shooting. Three died of starvation. The desperation is evident in Persson's diary: "School is closed, because the children are too weak or sick to attend. I spend most of the day in bed. I do not quite want to die. I am just not sure that I have it in me to live" (*The Diaries of Margareta Persson*, Umeå Heritage Museum, book 8, p. 65).

Then, early on Christmas morning, a stranger arrived. Ms. Persson writes,

We were lighting candles in the chapel. We had decided to keep our own little *julotta** here, as going to Varg-

* The main Christmas church service in Sweden at the time, held at 4:00 a.m. on Christmas Day.

fjärda was unthinkable. As we lit the candles, I heard song, and I saw someone standing at the pulpit. It was a man, all dressed in black. I cannot describe it properly, but he was singing to us, and it was as if my head brightened.

As the villagers filed into the chapel, the strange man proceeded to hold a Mass, of sorts.

Although the chapel is quite small, I could not see his face clearly. It was as if radiance obscured his features. He opened his mouth, and a sound both like and unlike song came out. I could not make out the words, but the song reached right into my chest and unraveled an ache I had not known was there. All around me, people were crying and laughing, screaming and moaning; we reached out to him like drowning children. He stepped down from the pulpit and moved among us, embracing us and laying his hands on us. He laid his arms around me; he smelled of myrrh and roses (*Diaries*, book 8, p. 73).

The priest earned the name *Sjungpastorn*, "the sing-pastor." He held Mass not only on Sunday mornings, but every single morning for the better part of a year. The Masses followed the same pattern as the first on Christmas morning: Sjungpastorn would stand at the pulpit and sing his wordless song, and the villagers sang along. At the end of the Mass, he would walk among the pews and touch or even embrace the people.

Ms. Persson doesn't describe the man in great detail. What she does say is very interesting, elaborating on her observation that she "could not see his face clearly": he was "not fully formed, like a clay doll or a new-born child" (*Diaries,* book 8, p. 95). Furthermore, the man doesn't speak, but produces other types of noise (the same type of phenomenon is described in Selma Lagerlöf's "En historia fran Långsjö,"[*] about the appearance of a strange-looking cow who couldn't moo). Lastly, being close to him creates an intense feeling of bliss, and he regularly *touches* the villagers. All these are characteristics of Pyret, and in chronicling them Ms. Persson finally gives us a possible clue to Pyret's procreation cycle.

In the autumn of 1868, Sjungpastorn began looking poorly and grayish. Ms. Persson mentions that he began touching people outside of Mass, specifically men. It didn't stop there. On the night of September 20, someone knocked on Margareta's door.

It was Emilia Magnusson, saying that Sjungpastorn had lain down with Olof Nilsson while Olof was sleeping. I said that Olof must have had a nightmare, but then Emilia told me that Olof's wife had been witness to it. She had been sitting with an ailing cow, and when she came into the bedroom saw Sjungpastorn in the bed, straddling her husband. She had fetched the farmhand, who had seen it too. They were afraid to intervene but made enough noise to wake Olof up, who then started screaming, and Sjungpastorn fled out a window and disappeared into the forest (*Diaries,* book 9, p. 82).

Sjungpastorn was never seen again. It does seem that he was nearing the end of his life cycle and therefore tried to

[*] Lagerlöf, Selma: *Troll och människor,* Albert Bonniers Boktryckeri, Stockholm, 1915, p. 95.

procreate; that he chose a man indicates that he was looking for sperm to fertilize an egg. There is no mention in Ms.
Persson's diaries of Pyret—perhaps because she didn't know
of the legend, or the villagers never made the connection.
After all, Sjungpastorn resembled a man and not a beast.

My Own Investigations into the Situation at "Lillbo"

So far, my findings have mostly fallen within the realm of
folklore, but I am about to present modern-day evidence that
we are not dealing with a cryptid but *a real being*. I have
previously stated that accounts of Pyret assuming human
form have been extremely rare. Recent events at the village
of "Lillbo" hint at a new development. While unraveling
Margareta Persson's account of Sjungpastorn, I met an informant at the Umeå Heritage Museum. A stocky woman in her
eighties, she worked as a volunteer at the museum. When she
heard about my area of research, she immediately asked me
to interview her. Please note that the informant's name and
the village's name have been changed for their protection.

Annika M was born in Lillbo in 1931, raising the population from thirty-five to thirty-six. Situated in the region of
Dalarna, the village had grown up around a foundry, which
was shut down in the early twentieth century. Like most of
her generation, Annika left in her teens to find work elsewhere, eventually settling in Umeå. She would not return to
Lillbo for thirty years. In a taped interview, Annika told me
of the events that took place when she finally did return.

It was in October 1978 when Annika's father unexpectedly called her. She hadn't spoken to her parents for several years, having broken off contact with them because she felt they were "bitter" and "stuck in the past." Now pensioners in their late sixties, they remained in Lillbo. Her father begged Annika to visit, although he wouldn't explain why: "My father had never talked to me like that before. I thought one of them must be ill or dying, so I got into my car and drove there as quickly as I could."

The village was no better than she remembered it, with "a single main street, a dirt road really ... some houses on each side of the road, and the little grocery store in the middle. The forest is littered with abandoned cottages." As she came to her parents' house, she quickly had the feeling that something was wrong.

I had been expecting them to be old and frail—sixty-seven was ancient to me then, you know—but they looked ... sort of plump and shiny. Like well-fed toddlers. And something was just *off*. Especially with Mother. She was sitting on the kitchen sofa with this stiff grin, almost from ear to ear. I thought, that's it. It's Alzheimer's.

Before Annika could greet her mother, her father pulled her with him into the living room and closed the door. In hushed tones, he told her a story.

A group of strangers had settled in the village some time ago. They didn't speak Swedish, but were light-skinned, so Father had thought maybe they were defectors from the USSR. "They came visiting all the time," he said. "We thought it was nice at first. They made you feel really good, you know? They made us feel young. But now we're prisoners." It made no sense. I asked him what was really going on, and what was wrong with Mother? He whispered, "That's not your mother. It won't let me leave. It's doing something to me at night. You have to get me out of here."

All of this sounded crazy to Annika, and to find time to think she "told them I had to go for a walk." She made her way down to the empty main street, where "The paint on the houses was chipped and fading, the stairs rotting; everything was falling apart." Soon, she noticed something odd.

I peeked into the grocery store and saw someone standing behind the counter, and a customer on the other side. Just what you might expect. But the customer would put some groceries on the counter, and after the cashier rang them up, the customer put the wares back on the shelves again! Then they started all over again. I looked while they did it four times. They were still doing it when I left.

As she went farther down the street, she happened upon a man chopping wood outside his house. Something wasn't quite right here, either:

I realized he wasn't really chopping anything. He was just moving his axe up and down, like a robot. I went closer, because his clothes looked strange—like he was wearing a cat suit painted like regular clothes. Then he looked up at me. His eyes were ink, just dots of ink.

I ran back to my parents' home, and Father was standing next to my car with a little satchel over his shoulder. He looked like a terrified schoolboy. I was going to say something to him, but then Mother came out onto the porch. It was still light out—I could see her face. It wasn't Mother. And then she opened her mouth. I can't describe the sound she made.

Annika got her father into the car and drove all the way back to Umeå without stopping. "We never came back to Lillbo. We never told anyone, because who would have believed us? Me and my father were the last, the last *people* to leave Lillbo."

Final Conclusions

As you might expect, Annika M's story prompted me to travel to Lillbo. Decades had passed since the events she described, but I still hoped to find clues, if not a live specimen. I also needed to see the site for myself. An inexperienced and frightened observer, Annika M had provided an account that was vague and skewed toward the monstrous. I, on the other hand, had studied Pyret for a very long time. I had nothing to fear from a creature I knew to be, in essence, benign.

I arrived at the village late in the afternoon. As it was October, I was treated to a spectacular turning of leaves. Annika had described the village as "falling apart" on her visit decades ago; now, the houses were practically rotting shells. I looked into windows and doorways where I could, but found nothing interesting . . . until I tried the door to the grocery store. It was half-stuck, but unlocked, and I managed to get it open.

Everyday objects filled the shelves on the walls: alarm clocks, stationery, china, clothes, silverware, paintings, lamps, scales, Bakelite telephones, canned goods, stuffed toys, sewing machines, picture frames. A powdery smell in the air made me think of plastic gone brittle in the sun. In the middle of the floor, its back to the counter, sat a molding velvet couch facing an old TV set. A little table to one side held a teapot, four cups, and a sheaf of paper. The couch was covered in a layer of something like hardened gelatin. That powdery smell became stronger as I drew closer, a taste of something like talcum settling on the tongue.

The paper on the table was inscribed with curlicued rows that resembled writing, but on closer inspection turned out to be just long loops of ink. A signature-like swirl sat in the bottom right corner. It looked very much like a childish imitation of a letter.

As I wandered along the carefully stacked shelves, the ordered clutter left behind, I found myself doubting the premise of my own research—and this elicited a strangely powerful reaction. I think it was due in part to the fact that I have studied Pyret for so long and was suddenly closer than I had ever been to finding tangible proof of its existence. But this proof, these leavings, was far beyond what I had expected to find.

I have in this essay offered the possibility of Pyret's sentience, but so far my research points to it really being a non-sentient animal—talented, yes, but an animal nonetheless. This room, which more than anything resembled a shrine to humanity, raised a new question—one that might not be answered until Pyret's next appearance.

When a creature chooses to die surrounded by keepsakes from a species to which it doesn't belong, leaving an imitation of language behind—has it acted out of instinct or intelligence?

Augusta Prima

AUGUSTA STOOD in the middle of the lawn with the croquet club in a two-handed grasp. She had been offered the honor of opening the game. Mnemosyne's prized croquet balls were carved from bone, with inlaid enamel and gold. The ball at Augusta's feet stared up at her with eyes of bright blue porcelain. An invitation to a croquet game in Mnemosyne's court was a wonderful thing. It was something to brag about. Those who went to Mnemosyne's games saw and were seen by the right people. Of course, they also risked utter humiliation and ridicule.

Augusta was sweating profusely. It trickled down between her breasts, eventually forming damp spots on the front of her shirt. She could feel a similar dampness spreading in the seat of her too-tight knee pants. More moisture ran down her temples, making tracks in the thick layers of powder. Her artful corkscrew curls were already wilting.

The other guests spread out across the lawn, waiting for her move. Everyone who meant something was here. Our

Lady Mnemosyne sat under a lace umbrella on her usual podium. Her chamberlain Walpurgis lounged in the grass in his white surtout, watching Augusta with heavy-lidded eyes. At his side, the twin lovers Vergilia and Hermine shared a divan, embracing as usual. Today one of them was dressed in a crinoline adorned with leaves; the other wore a dress made of gray feathers. Their page, a changeling boy in garish makeup, stood behind them holding a tray of drinks.

Farther away, Augusta's sister Azalea had grown tired of waiting. She had stripped naked next to a shrubbery, methodically plucking leaves off its branches. Everyone except Azalea was watching Augusta. The only sound was that of tearing leaves.

Augusta took a deep breath, raised her club, and swung it with a grunt. The ball flew in a high arc, landing with a crunch in the face of the twins' page, who dropped his tray and doubled over. The garden burst into cheers and applause. Mnemosyne smiled and nodded from her podium. Augusta had passed the test.

The game thus opened, the other guests threw themselves into play. In a series of magnificent hits, Walpurgis knocked out two pages who were carried off with crushed eyebrows, broken teeth, and bleeding noses. The twins were in unusually bad shape, mostly hitting balls instead of pages. Augusta played very carefully, focusing on not getting hit. There were a few breaks for cake, games, and flogging a servant. Finally, Hermine and Vergilia, one hand each on the club, hit Augusta's ball and it rolled well into the woods beyond the gardens. The hit was considered so stylish that Augusta was sent out of the game. She wandered in among the trees to find her ball.

Under one of the dog-rose bushes lay a human corpse: a man in a gray woolen suit. They sometimes wandered into the woods by mistake. This one had come unusually far. It was difficult to tell what had killed him. He had begun to putrefy; the swollen belly had burst his waistcoat open. A gold chain trailed from one of the pockets. Augusta bent forward, gingerly grasped the chain, and pulled it. A shiny locket emerged on the end of the chain, engraved with flowers. Augusta swung the locket up in the air and let it land in her palm. The touch sent a little chill along her arm, and for a moment she felt faint. She wrapped the locket in a handkerchief, put it in a pocket, and returned to the croquet green to announce that there was a new and interesting corpse.

Augusta returned to her rooms, a little medal pinned to her chest as thanks for her find. No one had noticed her taking the metal thing for herself. She shooed out her page and sat down on the bed to examine the thing further.

It seemed to be made of gold, engraved on both sides with flowery strands. It was heavy and cold in her palm. The vertigo gradually subsided, but the chills remained like an icy stream going from her hand to her neck. The chain attached to the locket by a little knob on the side. Another, almost invisible button sat across from it. She pressed it, and the locket sprung open to reveal a white disc painted with small lines. Three thin rods were attached to the center. One of them moved around the disc in twitching movements, making a ticking noise like a mouse's heart.

It was a machine. Augusta had seen things like it a few times, among the belongings of houses or humans who had been claimed by the gardens. They had always been broken, though. Mechanical things usually fell apart as soon as they came into the gardens' domain. It was a mystery how this thing could still be in one piece and working.

The chills had become an almost pleasant sensation. Augusta watched the rod chasing around the disc until she fell asleep.

She woke up in the same position as she'd fallen asleep in, on her side with the little machine in her hand. It was still now. Augusta frowned and called on her page. There were a handful of pages in the family, most of them nameless changelings raised in servitude. For various reasons, only two of them could carry a conversation, should one be so inclined. Augusta's page wasn't one of them.

"Fetch Azalea's page," she told him when he arrived.

Augusta watched the machine until there was a scratch at her door and Azalea's page stepped inside. He was a half-grown boy, with dark hair in oiled locks and eyes rimmed with kohl; a beautiful specimen that Azalea had insisted on taking into service despite his being too old to train properly. The boy stood in the middle of the room, having the audacity to stare directly at Augusta. She slapped him with the back of her hand. He shrunk back, turning his gaze to the floor. He walked over to the bed and started to remove his clothes.

"No, not now," Augusta said.

The boy froze halfway out of his surtout. Augusta tossed him the little locket.

"You will tell me what this is," she said.

"You don't know?" he said.

Augusta slapped him again.

"You will tell me what this is," she repeated.

He sniffled.

"It's a watch."

"And what does a watch do?"

"It measures time."

He pointed at the different parts of the watch, explaining their functions. The rods were called hands and chased around the clock face in step with time. The clock face indicated where in time one was located. It made Augusta shudder violently. Time was an abhorrent thing, a human thing. It didn't belong here. It was that power that made flesh rot and dreams wither. The gardens were supposed to lie beyond the grasp of time, in constant twilight; the sun just under the horizon, the moon shining full over the trees. Augusta told the boy as much:

"Time doesn't pass here. Not like that, not for us."

The boy twisted the little bud on the side of the locket, and the longest hand started to move again.

"But look," he said. "The hands are moving now. Time is passing now."

"But does it know how time flows? Does it measure time, or does it just move forward and call that time?"

The changeling stared at her.

"Time is time," he said.

Augusta cut his tongue out before she let him go. Azalea would be furious, but it was necessary.

She lay down on her bed again, but couldn't seem to fall

asleep. How could the hands on the watch keep moving here? The sun didn't go up or down. Didn't that mean time stood still here? It was common knowledge. Whenever one woke up, it was the same day as the day before.

She sat at her writing desk, jotting down a few things on paper. It made her head calm down a little. Then she opened a flask of poppy wine and drank herself back to sleep.

When Augusta woke up, her page was scratching at the door with a set of clothes in his arms and an invitation card between his teeth. It was an invitation to croquet. With a vague feeling that there was something she ought to remember, Augusta let the page dress and powder her.

She returned with a bump in the back of her head and a terrific headache. It had been a fantastic game. There had been gorging, Walpurgis had demonstrated a new dance, and the twins had—sensationally—struck each other senseless. Augusta had been behind everyone else in the game, eventually having her ball sent into the woods again, needing to go fetch it just like that time she'd found something under the dog-rose bush . . . under the dog-rose bush. She looked at her writing desk, where a little silk bundle sat on a piece of paper. She moved the bundle out of the way and read:

A minute is sixty seconds.
An hour is sixty minutes.
A day is twelve hours.
A day and a night is twenty-four hours.

Augusta opened the bundle and looked at the little locket. Some images appeared in her mind: Her first croquet game.

The corpse in the gray suit. The watch. The page who told her about time. A thirst to *know* how it worked. *What is time?* she wrote under the first note. *Is it here?*

Augusta took the watch and left her room. She wandered down to the orangery, which was lit from inside. Tendrils of steam rose from the roof. Inside, three enormous mounds lay on couches. The Aunts were as always immersed in their holy task to fatten. Three girls hovered around them, tiny in comparison. The girls were servants and successors, keeping the Aunts fed until they eventually perished, and then taking their places to begin the process anew. Augusta opened the watch, peeking at the clock face. The longest hand moved slowly, almost imperceptibly.

She walked from the orangery to the outskirts of the apple orchard, and from there to Porla's fen, then to the dog-rose shrubs in the woods outside Mnemosyne's court. Everywhere, the hands on the clock face moved, sometimes forward, sometimes backward. Sometimes they lifted from the clock face, hitting the glass protecting it, as if trying to escape.

Augusta woke up in Azalea's arms, under a canopy in Our Lady's arbor. The orgy they were visiting was still going on; there were low cries and the sound of breaking glass. Augusta couldn't remember what they had been doing, but she felt sore and bloated, and her sister was snoring very loudly. She was still wearing her shirt. Something rustled in her left breast pocket; she dug it out. It was a note. A little map, seemingly drawn in her own hand. Below the map was written a single sentence: *The places float just like time.* She had been wandering around, drawing maps and measuring distances. At some point. Mnemosyne's garden had first been on the right-hand side from Augusta's rooms. The next time she had found herself walking straight ahead to get there. The places floated. Augusta turned the note over. On the other side were the words: *Why is there time here? Why does it flow differently in different places? And if the places float, what is the nature of the woods?*

She returned to her rooms in a state of hangover. Papers were strewn everywhere it seemed: on and under the bed, on the dresser, in droves on the writing desk. Some of the notes were covered in dust. She couldn't remember writing some of them. But every word was in her own handwriting.

There was a stranger in Mnemosyne's court, towering over the other guests. She was dressed in simple robes, hooded and veiled, golden-yellow eyes showing through a thin slit. They shone down on Walpurgis, who made a feeble attempt to offer her a croquet club. Everyone else gave the stranger a wide berth.

"It is a djinneya. She is visiting Mnemosyne to trade information," the twins mumbled to Augusta.

"We wonder what information that is," Vergilia added.

"Those creatures know everything," Hermine said.

The djinneya sat by Mnemosyne's side during the whole game, seemingly deep in conversation with her hostess. Neither the twins' spectacular knockout of Walpurgis nor Azalea's attempt to throttle one of the pages caught her attention. Having been knocked out with a ball over her left knee, Augusta retreated to a couch, where she wrote an invitation.

· · ·

Augusta was woken at her writing desk by a knock at her door. A cloaked shape entered without asking permission. The djinneya seemed even taller indoors.

"Come in," said Augusta.

The djinneya nodded, unfastening the veil. Her skin was the color of fresh bruises. She grinned with a wide mouth, showing deep blue gums and long teeth filed into points.

"I thank you for your invitation, Augusta Prima."

She bent over Augusta's bed, fluffing the pillows, and sat down. A scent of sweat and spice spread in the room.

"You wanted to converse."

Augusta straightened, looking at the papers and notes on her desk. She remembered what it was she wanted to ask.

"You and your sort, you travel everywhere. Even beyond the woods. You know things."

The djinneya flashed her toothy smile.

"That we do."

"I would like to know the nature of time," Augusta said. "I want to know why time can't be measured properly here, and why everything moves around."

The djinneya laughed.

"Your kind doesn't want to know about those things. You can't bear it."

"But I do. I want to know."

The djinneya raised her thin eyebrows.

"Normally, you are tedious creatures," she said. "You only want trivial things. Is that person dead yet? Does this person still love that person? What did they wear at yesterday's party? I know things that could destroy worlds, and all you wish to know is if Karhu from Jumala is still unmarried."

She scratched her chin.

"I believe this is the first time one of your sort has asked me a good question. It's an expensive one, but I shall give you the answer. If you really are sure."

"I have to know," said Augusta. "What is the nature of the world?"

The djinneya smiled with both rows of teeth.

"Which one?"

Augusta woke up by the writing desk. The hangover throbbed behind her temples. She had fallen asleep with her head on an enormous stack of papers. She peered at it, leafing through the ones at the top. *There are eight worlds,* the first one said. *They lie side by side, in degrees of perfection. This world is the most perfect one.* Below these lines, written in a different ink, was: *There is one single world, divided into three levels that are partitioned off from one another by greased membranes.* Then in red ink: *There are two worlds and they overlap. The first is the land of Day, which belongs to the humans. The second is the land of Twilight, which belongs to the free folk, and of which the woods is a little backwater part. Both lands must obey Time, but the Twilight is ruled by the Heart, whereas the Day is ruled by Thought.* At the bottom of the page, large block letters proclaimed: *all of this is true.*

It dawned on Augusta that she remembered very clearly. The endless parties, in detail. The finding of the corpse, the short periods of clarity, the notes. The djinneya bending down to whisper in her ear.

. . .

A sharp yellow light stung Augusta's eyes. She was sitting at her writing desk in a very small room with wooden walls. A narrow bed with tattered sheets filled the rest of the space. The writing desk stood beneath a window. On the other side of the glass, the woods were bathed in light.

There was a door next to the bed. Augusta opened it, finding herself in a narrow hallway with another door at the end. A full-length mirror hung on the opposite wall. It showed a woman dressed in what had once been a blue surtout and knee pants. The fabrics were heavily stained with dirt and greenish mold and in some places worn through. Concentric rings of sweat radiated from the armpits. The shirt front was stiff with red and brown stains. Augusta touched her face. White powder lay in cracked layers along her nose and cheeks. Deep lines ran between her nose and mouth; more lines spread from the corners of her eyes. A golden chain hung from her breast pocket. She pulled on it, swinging the locket into her hand. It was ticking in a steady rhythm.

Augusta opened the other door and stepped out onto a landing. An unbearably bright light flooded over her. She backed into the hallway again, slamming the door.

"I told you. Your kind can't bear that question."

The djinneya stood behind her in the hallway, shoulders and head hunched under the low ceiling.

"What did you do?" Augusta said.

"What did *I* do? No. What did *you* do, Augusta Prima?"

She patted Augusta's shoulder.

"It started even before you invited me, Augusta Prima. You

tried to measure time in a land that doesn't *want* time. You tried to map a floating country."

The djinneya smiled.

"The woods spit you out, Augusta. Now you're in the land that measures time and draws maps."

Augusta gripped the hand on her shoulder.

"I want to go home. You have to take me home again."

"So soon? Well. All you have to do is forget what you have learned."

The djinneya squeezed past Augusta and stepped out onto the porch, where she stretched to her full height with a sigh.

"Good-bye, Augusta," she said over her shoulder. "And do try to hurry if you want to make it back. You're not getting any younger."

Aunts

IN SOME PLACES, time is a weak and occasional phenomenon. Unless someone claims time to pass, it might not, or does so only partly; events curl in on themselves to form spirals and circles.

The orangery is one such place. It is located in an apple orchard, which lies at the outskirts of a garden. The air is damp and laden with the yeasty sweetness of overripe fruit. Gnarled apple trees with bright yellow leaves flame against the cold and purpling sky. Red globes hang heavy on their branches. The orangery gets no visitors. The orchard belongs to a particular regent whose gardens are mostly populated by turgid nobles completely uninterested in the orchard. It has no servants, no entertainment. It requires walking, and the fruit is mealy.

But in the event someone did walk in among the trees, they would find them marching on for a very long time, every tree almost identical to the other. (Should that some-one try to count the fruit, they would also find that each tree has the exact same number of apples.) If this visitor did not turn around and flee for the safety of the more cultivated parts of the gardens, they would eventually see the trees disperse and the silver-and-glass bubble of an orangery rise out of the ground. Drawing closer, they would have seen this:

The insides of the glass walls were covered by a thin brown film of fat vapor and breath. Inside, fifteen orange trees stood along the curve of the cupola; fifteen smaller, potted trees made a circle inside the first. Marble covered the center, where three bolstered divans sat surrounded by low round tables. The divans sagged under the weight of three gigantic women.

The Aunts had one single holy task: to expand. They slowly accumulated layers of fat. A thigh bisected would reveal a pattern of concentric rings, the fat colored different hues. On the middle couch reclined Great-Aunt, who was the largest of the three. Her body flowed down from her head like waves of whipped cream, arms and legs mere nubs protruding from her magnificent mass.

Great-Aunt's sisters lay on either side. Middle Sister, her stomach cascading over her knees like a blanket, was eating little link sausages one by one, like a string of pearls. Little Sister, not noticeably smaller than the others, peeled the lid off a meat pie. Great-Aunt extended an arm, letting her fingers slowly sink into the pie's naked interior. She scooped up a fistful of dark filling and buried her face in it with a sigh. Little Sister licked the inside clean of the rest of the filling, then carefully folded it four times and slowly pushed it into her mouth. She snatched up a new link of sausages. She opened and scraped the filling from the skin with her teeth, then threw the empty skins aside. Great-Aunt sucked at the mouthpiece of a thin tube snaking up from a samovar on the table. The salty mist of melted butter rose up from the lid on the pot. She occasionally paused to twist her head and accept small marrow biscuits from one of the three girls hovering near the couches.

The gray-clad girls quietly moving through the orangery were Nieces. In the kitchens under the orangery, they baked sumptuous pastries and cakes; they fed and cleaned their Aunts. They had no individual names and were indistinguishable from one another, often even to themselves. The Nieces lived on leftovers from the Aunts: licking up crumbs mopped from Great-Aunt's chin, drinking the dregs of the butter samovar. The Aunts did not leave much, but the Nieces did not need much, either.

Great-Aunt could no longer expand, which was as it should be. Her skin, which had previously lain in soft folds around her, was stretched taut over the fat pushing outward from inside. Great-Aunt raised her eyes from her vast body and looked at her sisters, who each nodded in turn. The Nieces stepped forward, removing the pillows that held the Aunts upright. As she lay back, Great-Aunt began to shudder. She closed her eyes and her mouth became slack. A dark line appeared along her abdomen. As it reached her groin, she became still. With a soft sigh, the skin split along the line. Layer after layer of skin, fat, muscle, and membrane broke open until the breastbone was exposed and fell open with a wet crack. Golden blood washed out of the wound, splashing onto the couch and onto the floor, where it was caught in a shallow trough. The Nieces went to work, carefully scooping out organs and entrails. Deep in the cradle of her ribs lay a wrinkled pink shape, arms and legs wrapped around Great-

Aunt's heart. It opened its eyes and squealed as the Nieces lifted away the last of the surrounding tissue. They cut away the heart with the new Aunt still clinging to it, and placed her on a small pillow where she settled down and began to chew on the heart with tiny teeth.

The Nieces sorted intestines, liver, lungs, kidneys, bladder, uterus, and stomach; they were each put in separate bowls. Next they removed Aunt's skin. It came off easily in great sheets, ready to be cured and tanned and made into one of three new dresses. Then it was time for removing the fat: first the wealth of Aunt's enormous breasts, then her voluminous belly, her thighs; last, her flattened buttocks. The Nieces teased muscle loose from the bones; it needed not much force, but almost fell into their hands. Finally, the bones themselves, soft and translucent, were chopped up into manageable bits. When all this was done, the Nieces turned to Middle and Little Sister who were waiting on their couches, still and wide open. Everything neatly divided into pots and tubs; the Nieces scrubbed the couches and on them lay the new Aunts, each still busy chewing on the remains of a heart.

The Nieces retreated to the kitchens under the orangery. They melted and clarified the fat, ground the bones into fine flour, chopped and baked the organ meats, soaked the sweetbreads in vinegar, simmered the muscle until the meat fell apart in flakes, cleaned out and hung the intestines to dry. Nothing was wasted. The Aunts were baked into cakes and patés and pastries and little savory sausages and dumplings and crackling. The new Aunts would be very hungry and very pleased.

Neither the Nieces nor the Aunts saw it happen, but someone made their way through the apple trees and reached the orangery. The Aunts were getting a bath. The Nieces sponged the expanses of skin with lukewarm rose water. The quiet of the orangery was replaced by the drip and splash of water, the clunk of copper buckets, the grunts of Nieces straining to move flesh out of the way. They didn't see the curious face pressed against the glass, greasy corkscrew locks drawing filigree traces: a hand landing next to the staring face, cradling a round metal object. Nor did they at first hear the quiet, irregular ticking noise the object made. It wasn't until the ticking noise, first slow, then faster, amplified and filled the air that an Aunt opened her eyes and listened. The Nieces turned toward the orangery wall. There was nothing there, save for a handprint and a smudge of white.

Great-Aunt could no longer expand. Her skin was stretched taut over the fat pushing outward from inside. Great-Aunt raised her eyes from her vast body and looked at her sisters, who each nodded in turn. The Nieces stepped forward, removing the pillows that held the Aunts upright.

The Aunts gasped and wheezed. Their abdomens were a smooth, unbroken expanse: there was no trace of the telltale dark line. Great-Aunt's face turned a reddish blue as her own weight pressed down on her throat. Her shivers turned into convulsions. Then, suddenly, her breathing ceased altogether and her eyes stilled. On either side, her sisters rattled out their final breaths in concert.

The Nieces stared at the quiet bodies. They stared at one another. One of them raised her knife.

. . .

As the Nieces worked, the more they removed from Great-Aunt, the clearer it became that something was wrong. The flesh wouldn't give willingly but had to be forced apart. They resorted to using shears to open the rib cage. Finally, as they were scraping the last of the tissue from Great-Aunt's thigh bones, one of them said:

"I do not see a little Aunt."

"She should be here," said another.

They looked at each other. The third burst into tears. One of the others slapped the crying girl's head.

"We should look further," said the one who had slapped her sister. "She could be behind the eyes."

The Nieces dug further into Great-Aunt; they peered into her skull, but found nothing. They dug into the depths of her pelvis, but there was no new Aunt. Not knowing what else to do, they finished the division of the body, then moved on to the other Aunts. When the last of the three had been opened, dressed, quartered, and scraped, no new Aunt had yet been found. By now, the orangery's floor was filled with tubs of neatly ordered meat and offal. Some of the younger orange trees had fallen over and were soaking in golden blood. One of the Nieces, possibly the one who had slapped her sister, took a bowl and looked at the others.

"We have work to do," she said.

The Nieces scrubbed the orangery floor and cleaned the couches. They turned every last bit of the Aunts into a feast. They carried platters of food from the kitchens and laid it out on the surrounding tables. The couches were still empty. One of the Nieces sat down in the middle couch. She took a meat pastry and nibbled at it. The rich flavor of Great-Aunt's baked liver burst into her mouth; the pastry shell melted on her tongue. She crammed the rest of the pastry into her mouth and swallowed. When she opened her eyes, the other Nieces stood frozen in place, watching her.

"We must be the new Aunts now," the first Niece said.

One of the others considered this. "Mustn't waste it," she said eventually.

The new Aunts sat down on Middle Sister's and Little Sister's couches and tentatively reached for the food on the tables. Like their sister, they took first little bites, then bigger and bigger as the taste of the old Aunts filled them. Never before had they been allowed to eat from the tables. They ate until they couldn't down another bite. They slept. When they woke up, they fetched more food from the kitchen. The orangery was quiet save for the noise of chewing and swallowing. One Niece took an entire cake and buried her face in it, eating it from the inside out. Another rubbed marinated brain onto herself, as if to absorb it. Sausages, slices of tongue topped with jellied marrow, candied eyes that crunched and then melted. The girls ate and ate until the kitchen was empty and the floor covered in a layer of crumbs and drippings. They lay back on the couches and looked at one another's bodies, measuring bellies and legs. None of them were noticeably fatter.

"It's not working," said the girl on the leftmost couch. "We ate them all up and it's not working!" She burst into tears.

The middle girl pondered this. "Aunts can't be Aunts without Nieces," she said.

"But where do we find Nieces?" said the rightmost. "Where did we come from?" The other two were silent.

"We could make them," said the middle girl. "We are good at baking, after all."

And so the prospective Aunts swept up the crumbs from floor and plates, mopped up juices and bits of jelly, and returned with the last remains of the old Aunts to the kitchens. They made a dough and fashioned it into three girl-shaped cakes, baked them, and glazed them. When the cakes were done, they were a crisp light brown and the size of a hand. The would-be Aunts took the cakes up to the orangery and set them down on the floor, one beside each couch. They wrapped themselves in the Aunt-skins and lay down on their couches to wait.

Outside, the apple trees rattled their leaves in a faint breeze. On the other side of the apple orchard was a loud party, where a gathering of nobles played croquet with human heads, and their changeling servants hid under the tables, telling each other stories to keep the fear away. No sound of this reached the orangery, quiet in the steady gloom. No smell of apples snuck in between the panes. The Aunt-skins settled in soft folds around the sleeping girls.

Eventually one of them woke. The girl-shaped cakes lay on the floor, like before.

The middle girl crawled out of the folds of the skin dress and set her feet down on the floor. She picked up the cake sitting on the floor next to her.

"Perhaps we should eat them," she said. "And the Nieces will grow inside us." But her voice was faint.

"Or wait," said the leftmost girl. "They may yet move."

"They may," the middle girl said.

The girls sat on their couches, cradled in the skin dresses, and waited. They fell asleep and woke up again, and waited.

. . .

In some places, time is a weak and occasional phenomenon. Unless someone claims time to pass, it might not, or does so only partly; events curl in on themselves to form spirals and circles.

The Nieces wake and wait, wake and wait, for Aunts to arrive.

Jagannath

ANOTHER CHILD WAS BORN in the great Mother, excreted from the tube protruding from the Nursery ceiling. It landed with a wet thud on the organic bedding underneath. Papa shuffled over to the birthing tube and picked the baby up in his wizened hands. He stuck two fingers in the baby's mouth to clear the cavity of oil and mucus, and then slapped its bottom. The baby gave a faint cry.

"Ah," said Papa. "She lives." He counted fingers and toes with a satisfied nod. "Your name will be Rak," he told the baby.

Papa tucked her into one of the little niches in the wall where babies of varying sizes were nestled. Cables and flesh moved slightly, accommodating the baby's shape. A teat extended itself from the niche, grazing her cheek; Rak automatically turned and sucked at it. Papa patted the soft little head, sniffing at the hairless scalp. The metallic scent of Mother's innards still clung to it. A tiny flailing hand closed around one of his fingers.

"Good grip. You'll be a good worker," mumbled Papa.

. . .

Rak's early memories were of rocking movement, of Papa's voice whispering to her as she sucked her sustenance, the background gurgle of Mother's abdominal walls. Later, she was let down from the niche to the older children, a handful of plump bodies walking bow-legged on the undulating floor, bathed in the soft light from luminescent growths in the wall and ceiling. They slept in a pile, jostling bodies slick in the damp heat and the comforting rich smell of raw oil and blood.

Papa gathered them around his feet to tell them stories.

"What is Mother?" Papa would say. "She took us up when our world failed. She is our protection and our home. We are Her helpers and beloved children." Papa held up a finger, peering at them with eyes almost lost in the wrinkles of his face. "We make sure Her machinery runs smoothly. Without us, She cannot live. We only live if Mother lives."

Rak learned that she was a female, a worker, destined to be big and strong. She would help drive the peristaltic engine in Mother's belly, or work the locomotion of Her legs. Only one of the children, Ziz, was male. He was smaller than the others, with spindly limbs and bulging eyes in a domed head. Ziz would eventually go to the Ovary and fertilize Mother's eggs. Then he would take his place in Mother's head as pilot.

"Why can't we go to Mother's head?" said Rak.

"It's not for you," said Papa. "Only males can do that. That's the order of things: females work the engines and pistons so that Mother can move forward. For that, you are big and strong. Males fertilize Mother's eggs and guide Her. They need to be small and smart. Look at Ziz." Papa indicated the boy's thin arms. "He will never have the strength you have. He would never survive in the Belly. And you, Rak, will be too big to go to Mother's head."

Every now and then, Papa would open the Nursery door and talk to someone outside. Then he would collect the biggest of the children, give it a tight hug, and usher it out the door. The children never came back. They had begun work. Soon after, a new baby would be excreted from the tube.

When Rak was big enough, Papa opened the Nursery's sphincter door. On the other side stood a hulking female. She dwarfed Papa, muscles rolling under a layer of firm blubber.

"This is Hap, your caretaker," said Papa.

Hap held out an enormous hand.

"You'll come with me now," she said.

Rak followed her new caretaker through a series of corridors connected by openings that dilated at a touch. Dull metal cabling veined the smooth, pink flesh underfoot and around them. The tunnel was lit here and there by luminous growths, similar to the Nursery, but the light more reddish. The air became progressively warmer and thicker, gaining an undertone of something unfamiliar that stuck to the roof of Rak's mouth. Gurgling and humming noises reverberated through the walls, becoming stronger as they walked.

"I'm hungry," said Rak.

Hap scraped at the wall, stringy goop sloughing off into her hand.

"Here," she said. "This is what you'll eat now. It's Mother's food for us. You can eat it whenever you like."

It tasted thick and sweet sliding down her throat. After a few swallows Rak was pleasantly full. She was licking her lips as they entered the Belly.

More brightly lit and bigger than the Nursery, the chamber was looped through and around by bulging pipes of flesh. Six workers were evenly spaced out in the chamber, kneading the flesh or straining at great valves set into the tubes.

"This is the Belly," said Hap. "We move the food Mother eats through her entrails."

"Where does it go?" asked Rak.

Hap pointed to the far end of the chamber, where the bulges were smaller.

"Mother absorbs it. Turns it into food for us."

Rak nodded. "And that?" She pointed at the small apertures dotting the walls.

Hap walked over to the closest one and poked it. It dilated, and Rak was looking into a tube running left to right along the inside of the wall. A low grunting sound came from somewhere inside. A sinewy worker crawled past, filling up the space from wall to wall. She didn't pause to look at the open aperture.

"That's a Leg worker," said Hap. She let the aperture close and stretched.

"Do they ever come out?" said Rak.

"Only when they're going to die. So we can put them in the engine. Now. No more talking. You start over there." Hap steered Rak toward the end of the chamber. "Easy work."

Rak grew, putting on muscle and fat. She was one of twelve workers in the Belly. They worked and slept in shifts. One worked until tired, then ate, and then curled up in the sleeping niche next to whoever was there. Rak learned work songs to sing in time with the kneading of Mother's intestines, the turning of the valves. The eldest worker, an enormous female called Poi, usually led the chorus. They sang stories of how Mother saved their people. They sang of the parts of Her glorious body, the movement of Her myriad legs.

"What is outside Mother?" Rak asked once, curled up next to Hap, wrapped in the scent of sweat and oil.

"The horrible place that Mother saved us from," mumbled Hap. "Go to sleep."

"Have you seen it?"

Hap scoffed. "No, and I don't want to. Neither do you. Now quiet."

Rak closed her eyes, thinking of what kind of world might be outside Mother's body, but could only imagine darkness. The thought made a chill run down her back. She crept closer to Hap, nestling against her back.

The workload was never constant. It had to do with where Mother went and what she ate. Times of plenty meant hard work, the peristaltic engine swelling with food. But during those times, the females also ate well; the mucus coating Mother's walls grew thick and fragrant, and Rak would put on a good layer of fat. Then Mother would move on and the food would become less plentiful, Her innards thinning out and the mucus drying and caking. The workers would slow down, sleep more, and wait for a change. Regardless of how much there was to eat, Rak still grew, until she looked up and realized she was no longer so small compared to the others.

Poi died in her sleep. Rak woke up next to her cooling body, confused that Poi wasn't breathing. Hap had to explain that she was dead. Rak had never seen a dead person before. Poi just lay there, her body marked from the lean time, folds of skin hanging from her frame.

The workers carried Poi to a sphincter near the top of the chamber and dropped her into Mother's intestine. They took turns kneading the body through Mother's flesh, the bulge becoming smaller and smaller until Poi was consumed altogether.

"Go to the Nursery, Rak," said Hap. "Get a new worker."

Rak made her way up the tubes. It was her first time outside the Belly since leaving the Nursery. The corridors looked just like they had when Hap had led her through them long ago.

The Nursery looked much smaller. Rak towered in the opening, looking down at the tiny niches in the walls and the birthing tube bending down from the ceiling. Papa sat on his cot, crumpled and wrinkly. He stood up when Rak came in, barely reaching her shoulder.

"Rak, is it?" he said. He reached up and patted her arm. "You're big and strong. Good, good."

"I've come for a new worker, Papa," said Rak.

"Of course you have." Papa looked sideways, wringing his hands.

"Where are the babies?" she said.

"There are none," Papa replied. He shook his head. "There haven't been any . . . viable children, for a long time."

"I don't understand," said Rak.

"I'm sorry, Rak." Papa shrank back against the wall. "I have no worker to give you."

"What's happening, Papa? Why are there no babies?"

"I don't know. Maybe it is because of the lean times. But there have been lean times before, and there were babies then. And no visits from the Head, either. The Head would know. But no one comes. I have been all alone." Papa reached out for Rak, stroking her arm. "All alone."

Rak looked down at his hand. It was dry and light. "Did you go to the Head and ask?"

Papa blinked. "I couldn't do that. My place is in the Nursery. Only the pilots go to the Head."

The birthing tube gurgled. Something landed on the bedding with a splat. Rak craned her neck to look.

"But look, there's a baby," she said.

The lumpy shape was raw and red. Stubby limbs stuck out here and there. The head was too big. There were no eyes or nose, just a misshapen mouth. As Rak and Papa stared in silence, it opened its mouth and wailed.

"I don't know what to do," whispered Papa. "All the time, they come out like this."

He gently gathered up the malformed thing, covering its mouth with a hand until it stopped breathing. Tears rolled down his lined cheeks.

"My poor babies," said Papa.

As Rak left, Papa rocked the lump in his arms, weeping.

Rak didn't return to the Belly. She went forward. The corridor quickly narrowed, forcing Rak to a slow crawl on all fours. The rumble and sway of Mother's movement, so different from the gentle roll of the Belly, pressed her against the walls. Eventually, the tunnel widened into a round chamber. At the opposite end sat a puckered opening. On her right, a large round metallic plate was set into the flesh of the wall, the bulges ringing it glowing brightly red. Rak crossed the chamber to the opening on the other side. She touched it, and it moved with a groaning noise.

It was a tiny space: a hammock wrapped in cabling and tubes in front of two circular panes. Rak sat down in the hammock. The seat flexed around her, molding itself to her shape. The panes were streaked with mucus and oil, but she could faintly see light and movement on the other side. It made her eyes hurt. A tube snaked down from above, nudging her cheek. Rak automatically turned her head and opened her mouth. The tube thrust into her right nostril. Pain shot up between Rak's eyes. Her vision went dark. When it cleared, she let out a scream.

Above, a blinding point of light shone in an expanse of vibrant blue. Below, a blur of browns and yellows rolled past with alarming speed.

Who are you? a voice said. It was soft and heavy. *I was so lonely.*

"Hurts," Rak managed.

The colors and light muted, and the vision narrowed at the edges so that it seemed Rak was running through a tunnel. She unclenched her hands, breathing heavily.

Better?

Rak grunted.

You are seeing through my eyes. This is the outside world. But you are safe inside me, my child.

"Mother," said Rak.

Yes. I am your mother. Which of my children are you?

The voice was soothing, making it easier to breathe. "I'm Rak. From the Belly."

Rak, my child. I am so glad to meet you.

The scene outside rolled by: yellows and reds, and the blue mass above. Mother named the things for her. *Sky. Ground. Sun.* She named the sharp things scything out at the bottom of her vision: *mandibles* and the frenetically moving shapes glimpsed at the edges: *legs*. The cold fear of the enormous outside gradually faded in the presence of that warm voice. An urge to urinate made Rak aware of her own body again, and her purpose there.

"Mother. Something is wrong," she said. "The babies are born wrong. We need your help."

Nutrient and DNA deficiency, Mother hummed. *I need food.*

"But you can move everywhere, Mother. Why are you not finding food?"

Guidance systems malfunction. Food sources in the current area are depleted.

"Can I help, Mother?"

The way ahead bent slightly to the right. Mother was running in a circle.

There is an obstruction in my mainframe. Please remove the obstruction.

Behind Rak, something clanged. The tube slithered out of her nostril and she could see the room around her again. She turned her head. Behind the hammock a hatch had opened in the ceiling, the lid hanging down, rungs lining the inside. The hammock let Rak go with a sucking noise, and she climbed up the rungs.

Inside, gently lit in red, was Mother's brain: a small space surrounded by cables winding into flesh. A slow pulse beat through the walls. Half sitting against the wall was the emaciated body of a male. Its head and right shoulder were resting on a tangle of delicate tubes, bloated and stiff where they ran in under the dead male's body, thin and atrophied on the other. Rak pulled at an arm. Mother had started to absorb the corpse; it was partly fused to the wall. She tugged harder, and the upper body finally tore away and fell sideways. There was a rushing sound as pressure in the tubes evened out. The body was no longer in the way of any wires or tubes that Rak could see. She left it on the floor and climbed back down the hatch. Back in the hammock, the tube snuck into her nostril, and Mother's voice was in her head again.

Thank you, said Mother. *Obstruction has been removed. Guidance system recalibrating.*

"It was Ziz, I think," said Rak. "He was dead."

Yes. He was performing maintenance when he expired.

"Aren't there any more pilots?"

You can be my pilot.

"But I'm female," Rak said.

That is all right. Your brain gives me sufficient processing power for calculating a new itinerary.

"What?"

You don't have to do anything. Just sit here with me.

Rak watched as Mother changed course, climbing the wall of the canyon and up onto a soft yellow expanse: *Grassland,* Mother whispered. The sky sat heavy and blue over the grass. Mother slowed down, Her mouthpieces scooping up plants from the ground.

Angular silhouettes stood against the horizon.

"What is that?" said Rak.

Cities, Mother replied. *Your ancestors used to live there. But then the cities died, and they came to me. We entered an agreement. You would keep me company, and in exchange I would protect you until the world was a better place.*

"Where are we going?"

Looking for a mate. I need fresh genetic material. My system is not completely self-sufficient.

"Oh." Rak's mouth fell open. "Are there . . . more of you?"

Of sorts. There are none like me, but I have cousins that

roam the steppes. A sigh. *None of them are good company. Not like my children.*

Mother trundled over the grassland, eating and eating. Rak panicked the first time the sun disappeared, until Mother wrapped the hammock tight around her and told her to look up. Rak quieted at the sight of the glowing band laid across the sky. *Other suns,* Mother said, but Rak could not grasp it. She settled for thinking of it like lights in the ceiling of a great room.

They passed more of the cities: jagged spires and broken domes, bright surfaces crisscrossed with cracks and curling green. Occasionally flocks of other living creatures ran across the grass. Mother would name them all. Each time a new animal appeared, Rak asked if that was Her mate. The answer was always no.

"Are you feeling better?" Rak said eventually.

No. A sighing sound. *I am sorry. My system is degraded past the point of repair.*

"What does that mean?"

Good-bye, my daughter. Please use the exit with green lights.

Something shot up Rak's nostril through the tube. A sting of pain blossomed inside her forehead, and she tore the tube out. A thin stream of blood trailed from her nose. She wiped at it with her arm. A shudder shook the hammock. The luminescence in the walls faded. It was suddenly very quiet.

"Mother?" Rak said into the gloom. Outside, something was different. She peered out through one of the eyes. The world wasn't moving.

"Mother!" Rak put the tube in her nose again, but it fell out and lay limp in her lap. She slid out of the hammock, standing up on stiff legs. The hatch to Mother's brain was still open. Rak pulled herself up into the little space. It was pitch-dark and still. No pulse moved through the walls.

Rak left Mother's head and started down the long corridors, down toward the Nursery and the Belly. She scooped some mucus from the wall to eat, but it tasted rank. It was getting darker. Only the growths around the round plate between the Head and the rest of the body were still glowing brightly. They had changed to green.

In the Nursery, Papa was lying on his cot, chest rising and falling faintly.

"There you are," he said when Rak approached. "You were gone for so long."

"What happened?" said Rak.

Papa shook his head. "Nothing happened. Nothing at all."

"Mother isn't moving," said Rak. "I found Her head, and She talked to me, and I helped Her find her way to food, but She says She can't be repaired, and now She's not moving. I don't know what to do."

Papa closed his eyes. "Our Mother is dead," he whispered. "And we will go with Her."

He turned away, spreading his arms against the wall, hugging the tangle of cabling and flesh. Rak left him there.

In the Belly, the air was thick and rancid. The peristaltic engine was still. Rak's feet slapping against the floor made a very loud noise. Around the chamber, workers were lying along the walls, half-melted into Mother's flesh. The Leg accesses along the walls were all open; here and there an arm or a head poked out. Hap lay close to the entrance, resting on her side. Her body was gaunt, her ribs fully visible through the skin. She had begun sinking into the floor; Rak could still see part of her face. Her eyes were half-closed, as if she were just very tired.

Rak backed out into the corridor, turning back toward the Head. The sphincters were all relaxing, sending the foul air from the Belly toward her, forcing her to crawl forward. The last of the luminescence faded. She crawled in darkness until she saw a green shimmer up ahead. The round plate was still there. It swung aside at her touch.

The air coming in was cold and sharp, painful on the skin, but fresh. Rak breathed in deep. The hot air from Mother's insides streamed out above her in a cloud. The sun hung low on the horizon, its light far more blinding than Mother's eyes had seen it. One hand in front of her eyes, Rak swung her legs out over the rim of the opening and cried out in surprise when her feet landed on grass. The myriad blades prickled the soles of her feet. She sat there, gripping at the grass with her toes, eyes squeezed shut. When the light was less painful, she opened her eyes a little and stood up.

The aperture opened out between two of Mother's jointed legs. They rested on the grass, each leg thicker around than Rak could reach with her arms. Beyond them, she could glimpse more legs to either side. She looked up. Behind her, the wall of Mother's body rose up, more than twice Rak's own height. Beyond the top there was sky, a blue nothing, not flat as seen through Mother's eyes but deep and endless. In front of her, the grassland, stretching on and on. Rak held on to the massive leg next to her. Her stomach clenched, and she bent over and spat bile. There was a hot lump in her chest that wouldn't go away. She spat again and knelt on the grass.

"Mother," she whispered in the thin air. She leaned against the leg. It was cold and smooth. "Mother, please." She crawled in under Mother's legs, curling up against Her body, breathing in Her familiar musk. A sweet hint of rot lurked below. The knot in Rak's chest forced itself up through her throat in a howl.

Rak eventually fell asleep. She dreamed of legs sprouting from her sides, her body elongating and dividing into sections, taking a sinuous shape. She ran over the grass, legs in perfect unison, muscles and vertebrae stretching and becoming powerful. The sky was no longer terrible. Warm light caressed the length of her scales.

A pattering noise in the distance woke her up. Rak stretched and rubbed her eyes. Her cheeks were crusted with salt. She scratched at her side. An itching line of nubs ran along her ribs. Beside her, Mother's body no longer smelled of musk; the smell of rot was stronger. She crawled out onto the grass and rose to her feet. The sky had darkened, and a pale orb hung in the void, painting the landscape in stark gray and white. Mother lay quiet, stretched out into the distance. Rak saw now that Mother's carapace was gray and pitted, some of the many legs cracked or missing.

In the bleak light, a long shape on many legs approached. When it came close, Rak saw it was much smaller than Mother—perhaps three or four times Rak's length. She stood very still. The other paused a few feet away. It reared up,

forebody and legs waving back and forth. Its mandibles clat-
tered. Something about its movement caused a warm stirring
in Rak's belly. After a while, it turned around, depositing a
gelatinous sac on the ground. It slowly backed away.

Rak approached the sac. It was the size of her head. Inside,
a host of little shapes wriggled around. Her belly rumbled.
The other departed, mandibles clattering, as Rak ripped the
sac open with her teeth. The wriggling little things were
tangy on her tongue. She swallowed them whole.

She ate until she was sated, then crouched down on the
ground, scratching at her sides. Her arms and legs tingled.
She had a growing urge to run and stretch her muscles: to
run and never stop.

Transposing Worlds

The decision to translate my own work was born out of an old dream. When I first got serious about writing, I fantasized about becoming so well-known in Sweden that someone would translate my work into other languages. I put the thought out of my mind—I wasn't even published in Swedish yet—and ten years passed.

My country has a long and solid tradition when it comes to short stories and speculative fiction, but it proved difficult to publish either. Among the handful of Swedish magazines that published short stories, few were interested in the fantastic, and those that were died off one by one. Abroad, on the other hand, *Weird Tales* beckoned. And *Interzone, Asimov's, Strange Horizons.* Scores of magazines, just out of reach.

I was by no means sure my English was good enough. I pretended it was, figured I'd need some immersive practice, and applied to the Clarion SF & Fantasy Writers' Workshop on a lark. I got in, and ever since I've been writing stories in both Swedish and English, creating translations in both languages.

My experience of English reflects that of most Swedes of my generation. I studied British English from the fourth grade, learning through songs by the Beatles and the rituals of teatime. American English was the language of MTV and the movies, and, later, science fiction paperbacks. Being so exposed to both varieties, neither of which is your own, makes it difficult if not impossible to keep track of what word (and often, pronunciation) belongs where. You make do with the resulting composite. This collection may reflect that wonderful confluence and confusion.

Writing in Swedish and English are two very different experiences. Your native language resonates in your bones. Each spoken word reaffirms or changes the world as you see it, intellectually and emotionally. Because Swedish is my mother tongue, I can take enormous liberties with it because I know exactly and instinctively how it works. English doesn't quite allow itself to be grabbed by the scruff of its neck in the same way. As a result, I'm more careful with the prose, perhaps less adventurous, because without that gut reaction it's hard to know exactly how something will resonate with an English-speaking reader. On the other hand, I may find paths into English that a native speaker might not, because there are aspects of your native tongue that you just don't see, since you are standing in the middle of it. I am reminded of those times I've been amazed by how a non-native speaker can bend my own language in unexpected directions, or just approach it with an ear that makes it seem like a new creation.

Concepts and stories definitely work in different ways, depending on language. For example, "Jagannath" and "Aunts" *taste* different, partly because of the sound of words associated with the stories. They are both concerned with anatomy, and the English terms I found appropriate were often softer and less abrupt. The word *flesh*, for example, can be drawn out and rolls around in the mouth; the Swedish analogue *kött* (sounds similar to the English *shut*) is hard and brutal in comparison, and also means "meat," which is not the feel I wanted. The same goes for *intestine* versus *tarm*, *blubber* versus *späck*, and so on, with the exception of *slemhinna*, which sounds far better than *mucous membrane*.

Some concepts and cultural overtones refuse translation, but that's the case with any language. If I say something has a "dansband" atmosphere, a Swede will immediately know what I'm talking about and probably cringe. Few people outside Scandinavia will be familiar with the sickly sweet faux-country music played by men in identical frilly pastel suits and the claustrophobic image of small-town monoculture that comes with it (whether that culture actually exists is uncertain, but the cliché certainly does). So in these stories I've left in some words that could technically be translated but would completely lose their meaning. On the other hand, some small details have to be translated—even if some nuance is lost—because they aren't vital to the story and would just trip up the reader. In "Rebecka," there's a group of kids dressed in ski overalls that in Swedish would have been *bävernylon*: beaver nylon, a fabric so strong that you could be dragged behind a car without getting a scratch. The image of kids in beaver nylon overalls is a sort of shorthand for innocent childhood and everyday Sweden. Figuring out which of these concepts require translation and which do not has been a great exercise for understanding my own language. Cultural shorthand is convenient but can also make you a little sloppy, so being forced to think about what a throwaway phrase really means jolts you out of writing on autopilot.

It's inevitable, I suppose, that I've been told that my stories in English have a distinctly Nordic feel. It's not something I set out to achieve, but there are concepts that I do like to examine and play with and that I suppose are very Swedish—or Nordic, really. National identity is an artificial exercise, and the borders between the Nordic countries blur. But accepting the notion for a moment: "Some Letters for Ove Lindström" deals with being a child of the prog generation: the intellectual left of the seventies for whom the personal was political, who idealized a working class they didn't belong to, and who founded the image of the soft Swedish dad. The ultrastereotypical rituals of "Brita's Holiday Village" is another: the midsummer feast, dansband, the summer-dress-and-knitted-cardigan outfits of chilly Swedish summer. Both stories, I suppose, are about cultural identity.

This quality also comes through in the atmosphere of the stories. One sensation peculiar to the Nordic culture of my upbringing is that we really do live on the edge of fairy country. With a small population that's mostly gathered in towns, vast stretches of countryside could contain any number of critters. Many folktales, and other stories I grew up with, such as the ones by Finno-Swedish author Tove Jansson, show reality as a thin veneer behind which strange creatures move. I learned to be aware of things lurking in dark corners, of the *huldra* that looks human from the front but is a rotten tree at the back; of the *hattifatteners* gathering on hills to feed on thunderstorms. Weird fiction, when I discovered it, fit right into this worldview. Maybe a bit too much so, at the beginning: I was fifteen years old when I devoured all of H. P. Lovecraft's translated works in two weeks and had a short but near-psychotic revelation that all of it was true. I recovered, but reality still has a bit of a wobble.

And then there's the melancholy. The beloved Swedish word *vemod* is difficult to translate, but think of it as a wistful sorrow about something that is over or a quiet longing for something else. As a friend of mine put it, "smiling through tears." It shines through in much of our culture, a moody Bergman sibling in the backseat of the Volvo, sighing at the sunset.

I have tried to convey all of these things, and more. Hopefully some of them made it across to you.

—Karin Tidbeck, August 2012

ACKNOWLEDGMENTS

No writer works in a vacuum. These stories were written over the course of ten years, with the help and support from my family, friends, editors, fellow writers, critique groups, and teachers. Putting together *Jagannath*, I owe thanks to Robin Steen for his unwavering support and willingness to read anything I put in front of him at a moment's notice; to my fellow alumni of Clarion UCSD 2010; and to Ann and Jeff Vandermeer, Jeremy Zerfoss, and Teri Goulding for all their hard work with the first edition of *Jagannath*. Thanks also go out to my agent, Renee Zuckerbrot, and Tim O'Connell, Russell Perreault, and Mandy Licata at Vintage. I am profoundly grateful to you all.

PERMISSIONS

"Beatrice," from *Vem är Arvid Pekon?*, originally published in Sweden as "Beatrice" by Man av Skugga förlag, Gothenburg, in 2010. English translation published in *Steampunk Revolution* by Tachyon Publications, San Francisco, in 2012.

"Some Letters for Ove Lindström," from *Vem är Arvid Pekon?*, originally published in Sweden as "Några brev till Ove Lindström" by Man av Skugga förlag, Gothenburg, in 2010. English translation published in *Shimmer* (Number 14) in 2010.

"Miss Nyberg and I," from *Vem är Arvid Pekon?*, originally published in Sweden as "Fröken Nyberg och jag" by Man av Skugga förlag, Gothenburg, in 2010. This translation first published in English in *Jagannath* by Cheeky Frawg Books, Tallahassee, Florida, in 2012.

"Rebecka," from *Vem är Arvid Pekon?*, originally published in Sweden as "Rebecka" by Man av Skugga förlag, Gothenburg, in 2010. First appeared on Sourze.se in 2002 under the title "Samtal med Rebecka." This translation first published in English in *Jagannath* by Cheeky Frawg Books, Tallahassee, Florida, in 2012.

"Herr Cederberg," from *Vem är Arvid Pekon?*, originally published in Sweden as "Herr Cederberg" by Man av Skugga förlag, Gothenburg, in 2010. First appeared in *Ordkonst 1* in 2007 under the title "Att vara en humla." This translation first published in English in *Jagannath* by Cheeky Frawg Books, Tallahassee, Florida, in 2012.

"Who Is Arvid Pekon?," from *Vem är Arvid Pekon?*, originally published in Sweden as "Arvid Pekon" by Man av Skugga förlag, Gothenburg, in 2010. First appeared in *Jules Verne-Magasinet 513* in 2002 under the title "Vem är Arvid Pekon?" This translation first published in English in *Jagannath* by Cheeky Frawg Books, Tallahassee, Florida, in 2012.

"Brita's Holiday Village," from *Vem är Arvid Pekon?*, originally published in Sweden as "Tant Britas stugby" by Man av Skugga förlag, Gothenburg, in 2010. This translation first published in English in *Jagannath* by Cheeky Frawg Books, Tallahassee, Florida, in 2012.

"Reindeer Mountain" previously unpublished in Swedish or English.

"Cloudberry Jam" first appeared in English in *Unstuck Journal* (Number 1) in 2011. Swedish translation published under the title "Blodsband" by Mix Förlag, Stockholm, in 2011.

"Pyret" first published in English in *Jagannath* by Cheeky Frawg Books, Tallahassee, Florida, in 2012.

"Augusta Prima" first appeared in Sweden as "Augusta Prima" in *Mitrania* (Number 3) in 2009. English translation first appeared in *Weird Tales* (Number 357) in 2011.

"Aunts" first appeared in Sweden as "Tanterna" in *Insulae,* ed. Skurups folkhögskola in 2007. English translation published in *ODD?* in 2011.

"Jagannath" first appeared in English in *Weird Tales* (Number 358) in 2011. Swedish translation published under the same title by Mix förlag, Stockholm, in 2011.